EERIE

EERIE copyright © 2012 by Blake Crouch & Jordan Crouch
Cover copyright © 2012 by Jeroen ten Berge

EERIE is a work of fiction. Names, characters, places and incidents are either products of the authors' imaginations or used fictitiously. Any resemblance to actual events, locales, or persons, living or dead, is entirely coincidental. All rights reserved. No part of this publication may be reproduced or transmitted in any form or by any means, electronic or mechanical, without permission in writing from
Blake Crouch and Jordan Crouch.

For more information about Blake Crouch,
please visit www.blakecrouch.com.

For more information about Jordan Crouch,
please visit www.authorjordancrouch.com.

About EERIE

From newcomer Jordan Crouch and Blake Crouch, author of the runaway bestseller RUN, comes EERIE, a chilling, gothic thriller in the classic tradition of The Shining and The Sixth Sense.

TRAPPED INSIDE A HOUSE

On a crisp autumn evening in 1980, seven-year-old Grant Moreton and his five-year-old sister Paige were nearly killed in a mysterious accident in the Cascade Mountains that left them orphans.

WITH A FRIGHTENING POWER

It's been thirty years since that night. Grant is now a detective with the Seattle Police Department and long estranged from his sister. But his investigation into the bloody past of a high-class prostitute has led right to Paige's door, and what awaits inside is beyond his wildest imagining.

OVER ANYONE WHO ENTERS

His only hope of survival and saving his sister will be to confront the terror that inhabits its walls, but he is completely unprepared to face the truth of what haunts his sister's brownstone.

EERIE

A THRILLER

BLAKE CROUCH & JORDAN CROUCH

You don't have a soul. You are a Soul. You have a body.

—C.S. Lewis

OCTOBER 1980

"How much longer, Daddy?" Grant Moreton asks from the backseat of the '74 Impala. The boy catches a glimpse of his father's eyes in the rearview mirror. They aren't angry or even stern. Just tired and sad—the way they've looked for the past year.

"We're five minutes closer than the last time you asked. Do you remember how long I said it would be then?"

"Twenty minutes?"

"That's right. So what's twenty minus five?"

Grant glances over at the girl with braided pigtails sitting beside him. He is two years older than Paige, but his five-almost-six-year-old sister already understands math in a way he never will.

"What is it?" he whispers. "What's the answer?"

"No cheating," their father says. "Your sister helps out too much with your homework as it is."

Grant stares through the window as he tries to calculate the answer. There are mountains out there, but nothing to see at this time of night beyond the occasional glint of light from a distant house or a passing car.

On the radio: game six of the World Series. The Phillies are on the brink of beating the Kansas City Royals and the roar of the crowd comes like white noise through the speakers.

Grant feels a thump on the side of his leg. He looks over. Paige leans in, whispers, "It's fifteen."

He glances at the rearview to make sure their father hasn't noticed this treason.

"Fifteen," he says.

"You sure about that?"

Grant shoots her a sidelong look.

She responds with an almost imperceptible nod.

"I'm sure."

"That's right. Nice job, Paige."

Grant flushes with embarrassment, but in the mirror, his father's eyes are gentle.

"No worries, kiddo. That's what sisters are for."

Jim Moreton rolls down his window and flicks his cigarette outside. Grant glances back, watches it hit the pavement in a spray of sparks.

A sharp chilled blast of Douglas-fir fills the car.

They ride on in silence listening to the game.

Through the windshield, the road ahead of them winds, steadily climbing, the double yellow emerging out of nothing into the burn of the headlights.

The boy rests his head against the window. He shuts his eyes and retrieves the square of fabric from his pocket. Brings it to his nose. Breathes in the smell of his mother's nightgown. If he closes his eyes, he can almost pull the scene together, the way it should be—her in the passenger seat, his father's arm stretched across the back of her headrest. Grant is having a harder time picturing her face lately without help from a photograph, but the timbre of her voice retains sharper and truer than ever. If she were in the car right now, she'd be talking over the game. Playfully arguing with Jim about the volume of the radio, how fast he was driving, the graceless way he slingshots the car through each hairpin turn. Grant opens his eyes, and even though he knows she won't be there, the shock of the empty seat still registers.

Just fifteen minutes until we're there.

More than a year has passed since their last visit to the cabin, and so much changed it's like the memory belongs to someone else. They had driven up into the Cascades in the middle of summer. Their family place backed up to a small pond that stayed cold even through July. They'd stayed a month there. Days fishing and swimming. Hide-and-seek in the groves of hemlock that surrounded the property. The cold nights spent reading and playing games by the fireplace. It had been his and Paige's job every afternoon to gather sticks and fir cones to use as kindling.

Everything about that summer is so clear in his mind. Everything except for the little boy, because *he* had a mother and Grant doesn't and it hurts to remember.

"All right, here we go," Jim Moreton says, turning up the volume on the radio, the crowd-roar swelling. "Bases loaded. Come on, Phillies. Willie's got nothin'."

Grant has no idea who his father is talking about, just knows that he's done little else but watch baseball this last, awful year.

"My ears hurt, Dad," he says.

"Mine too," Paige echoes.

Grant's father opens the center console and fishes through its contents until he finds an old pack of spearmint gum.

"Chew this. It'll help."

He passes two sticks back to the children.

A moment later, he forces a yawn and unwraps one for himself.

"Pay attention, guys," he says through a mouthful of fresh gum. "You'll remember this game one day."

As a man, Grant will know everything there is to know about this game. It will assume an epic aura, in particular these final moments, this last at bat—Tug McGraw throwing to Willie Wilson, Phillies up three, but the bases loaded—Kansas City one swing away from total defeat or the comeback of the century.

Years later, Grant will watch the last strike on a videotape. See Willie Wilson swing and miss, thinking how strange it is to know what was happening to that '74 Impala, to his father, his sister, himself, on a remote highway in Washington State at the exact moment Tug threw his arms into the air and danced off the pitcher's mound, a World Series champion.

Riding in the backseat of the car as the world waits for the final pitch, Grant sees the headlights fire to life a sign on the side of the highway.

Stevens Pass
Elevation 4061

But the pitch never comes.

There is no end to the game.

Grant is trying to slide the patch of his mother's nightgown back into his pocket when Paige screams. He looks up, aA wall of blinding light pouring through the windshield. As the tires begin to screech, he's thrown violently against his sister who crashes into the door. The last thing he sees is the guardrail racing toward them, glowing brighter and brighter as the headlights close in.

The violence of the bumper punching through is cataclysmic, and then the noise drops away.

No sound but the revving engine.

Tires spinning like mad and nothing underneath them.

Grant's stomach lifts with the same weightless ache he experienced the time he rode a roller coaster.

The radio is still on, the airwaves now riddled with static.

The play-by-play announcer, whose name Grant will one day learn is Joe Garagiola, says, "The crowd will tell you what happens."

Paige says, "Daddy?"

Their father says, "Oh shit."

Grant opens his eyes.

The engine is hissing and the tires still barely spinning—above him.

The Impala is inverted. The radio gone silent. One headlight is busted; the other blazes intermittently. Through the fractured windshield, he sees the beam shining into an upside-down forest where mist lingers between the tall, straight trunks.

An image that will haunt him to the end of his days.

He calls out to his father.

Jim Moreton doesn't answer. He's crumpled into the steering column, the side of his face gleaming with blood and sparkling with bits of glass.

He is so terribly still.

Grant looks over at his sister. Like him, she hangs by her lap belt. Grant reaches down, unfastens his, and falls onto the ceiling, crying out as a flare of pain rides up the bone of his left leg.

Tears stream down his face.

His head throbs.

"Paige?"

She groans. He's lying under her now. Reaching up, he takes hold of her hand and gives it a squeeze.

"Paige, can you hear me?"

It's too dark to see if her eyes are open.

"What happened?" she asks quietly.

Something wet is dripping on his face.

"We wrecked."

"My chest hurts."

"It's okay, Paigy."

"It hurts really bad. Why are we upside down? Daddy?"

No answer.

"Daddy?"

"He's hurt," Grant says.

Her voice kicks up an octave. "Daddy?"

"It's gonna be okay," Grant says, though he has no idea if there's even a shred of truth to the statement.

"I want my daddy."

"He can't hear you right now, Paige."

"Is he dead?"

That possibility hasn't occurred to Grant until this moment.

"Touch him," she cries. "Make him answer."

Grant turns his attention to the front seat. His father is upside down, still buckled in, a string of blood dripping from the corner of his mouth onto the roof. The boy reaches out, touches his father's shoulder.

"Dad?"

His father makes no response.

Grant strains to hear if he's breathing, but the noise of the spinning tires and the hiss of the dying engine make it impossible to tell.

"Dad," he whispers. "Wake up."

"Is he alive?" Paige begs.

"I don't know."

She begins to cry.

Hysterical.

"It's gonna be all right," Grant says.

"No," she screams.

Grant leans in closer. He will never forget the smell of blood.

"Dad," he whispers. "It's Grant."

His father's hands still clench around the steering wheel. "Please do something if … if you're okay. If you can hear me. Just make a sound."

He will never recover from the silence.

"What's happening, Grant?"

"I don't know."

"Is Daddy okay?"

The tears are coming. Grant tries to hold back the sob, but there's no stopping it. He lies on the glass-covered roof and cries with his sister for a long time.

The engine has gone silent.

The last spinning wheel creaked to a halt.

Cold mountain air streams in through the busted windows.

Grant has unbuckled his sister and helped her out of the seat, and now they lie side-by-side on the roof, huddled together and shivering.

The air becomes redolent of wet evergreen trees. Rain is falling, pattering on the pine-needled floor of the forest and on the Impala's undercarriage.

The headlight dims away, now just a feeble swath of light.

The boy has no concept of how long they've been upended on this mountainside.

"Can you check Dad again?" Paige asks.

"I can't move my leg anymore."

"Why?"

"It hurts a lot and it's stiff."

In the darkness, the boy finds his sister's hand and holds it.
"Do you think Daddy's dead?" she asks.
"I don't know."
"Are we going to die?"
"Someone will find us."
"But what if they don't come?"
"Then I'll crawl up the mountain and find someone myself."
"But your leg is hurt."
"I can do it if I have to."
"What's it called," she says, "when you don't have a mom or a dad?"
"Orphan."

Grant braces against another push of fear-fueled emotion. So many questions springing up he feels like he's drowning.

Where will they live?
Who will pay for their food?
Their clothes?
Will he have to get a job?
Who will make them go to bed?
Who will fix their meals?
Make them eat good food?
Who will make them go to school?

"Is that what we are now, Grant?" Paige asks. "Are we orphans?"
"No, we're brother and sister, Paige."
"What if—"
"No matter what happens, I'll take care of you."
"But you're only seven."
"So?"
"You don't even know how to add."
"But you do. And I can do the other stuff. We can help each other. Like how Mom and Dad did."

Grant turns over in the dark, his face inches away from Paige's. Her breath smells faintly of spearmint gum. It warms his face sweetly.

"Don't be scared, Paige."
"But I am." Her voice breaks.
"I won't let anything happen to you."

"You promise?"

"I promise."

"Swear."

"I swear to you, Paige. I'll protect you."

"Will we still live in our house?"

"Of course. Where else would we live? It'll be just like it was only I'll be taking care of you."

She draws in a labored wheeze.

"It hurts when I breathe."

"Then don't breathe hard."

Grant wants to call out to their father again, but he fears it might upset her.

"I'm cold, Grant."

"Me too."

"How long until someone finds us?"

"They'll be here soon. Do you want to hear a story while we wait?"

"No."

"Not even your favorite?"

"Which one?"

"The one about the crazy scientist in the castle on the hill."

"It's too scary."

"You always say that. But this one's different."

Through the windshield, the beam of light has weakened such that it only offers a yellowed patch of illumination on the nearest tree.

"How is it different?"

"I can't just tell you. It'll ruin it."

"Okay." Paige moves in closer.

Outside, the headlight expires.

Pitch black inside the car now.

The rain is falling harder, and for a moment, Grant is paralyzed by the horror of it all.

"Come on," Paige says.

She nudges him in the dark.

Grant begins, his voice unsteady: "Once upon a time, there was a little girl named Paige."

"Just like me?"
"Just like you. And she had an older brother named Grant."
"Just like you."
He blinks through the tears reforming in his eyes.
Fights through the tremor in his voice.
Don't cry.
The mantra for a lifetime.
"Yes, just like me."
"Did they have parents?"
Everything inside the car is terribly still, but the woods around them have become alive in the silence. Rain pelts the carpet of leaves on the forest floor. Things snap in the darkness. The hoot of a lonesome owl goes unanswered.

The world outside is huge—so many things for a little boy to be afraid of.

"No. Paige and Grant lived in a beautiful house all by themselves, and they were very brave."

Thirty-One Years Later

Chapter 1

"Where'd you go for lunch?" Sophie asked.

Grant shook his head as he typed *Benjamin Seymour* and *Seattle* into the Google query box.

"I'm not playing this game."

"Come on. Don't make me go through your receipts."

"Will my participation in this conversation make it end sooner?"

"The Panda Express at Northgate?"

"Nope."

"Subway?"

Grant frowned at his partner across the border fence that divided their desks into equal surface areas—two messy inboxes, stacks of files, blank narrative forms, expense reports, a shared, miniature artificial Christmas tree.

"Subway it was." Sophie scribbled on a pad. She looked good today—a charcoal-colored pantsuit with a lavender blouse and a matching necklace, turquoise with silver fringing. She was of African and Native American descent. Sometimes, Grant thought he could see the Cherokee lineage in her dark almond eyes and hair so purely straight and black it shimmered like the blued steel of his service carry, an H&K P2000. They'd been working together since Benington had transferred to the North precinct two years ago.

"What are you writing down?" Grant asked.

"Keep in mind I haven't adjusted for wherever you eat on the weekends, but so far this year, I have seventy-nine documented visits to Subway."

"That's the best detective work I've ever seen you do, Benington."

"Got a few more numbers for you."

Grant surrendered, setting his work aside.

"Fine. Let's hear them."

"Forty. Three hundred sixteen. And, oh my God, one thousand five hundred eighty."

"Never mind, I don't want to know this."

"Forty is the approximate time in minutes you've waited while they toasted your sandwich, three hundred sixteen is the number of cheese slices you've eaten this year, and finally, one thousand five hundred eighty little round meat shapes have given their lives during the spicy Italian genocide of twenty-eleven."

"Where did you get those numbers?"

"Google and basic math. Does Subway sponsor you?"

"It's a solid restaurant," Grant said, turning back to his computer.

"It's not a restaurant."

On the far side of the room, he could hear the sergeant chewing someone's ass through the telephone. Otherwise, the cluster of desks and cubes stood mostly empty. The only other detective on the floor was Art Dobbs, the man on a much quieter, more civilized phone call.

Grant studied his search results which had returned a hundred thousand hits.

"Damn," he said.

"What?"

"Getting no love on my search. Guy was pretty quiet for a big spender."

Grant appended the word *attorney* to the string and tried again.

Just twenty-eight hundred hits this time, the first page dominated by Seymour's firm's website and numerous legal search engine results.

"*Was?*" Sophie said. "That's kind of cold."

"He's been missing …" Grant glanced at his watch "… forty-nine hours."

"Still possible he just left town and didn't feel like telling the world."

"No, I spoke with a few of his partners this morning. They described him as a man who played hard but worked even harder. He had a trial scheduled to begin this morning and I was assured that Seymour never let his extracurriculars interfere with work. He's one of Seattle's preeminent trial lawyers."

"I never heard of him."

"That's 'cause he does civil litigation."

"Still say he went off on a bender. Probably licking his wounds as we speak in some swank hotel."

"Well, I find it interesting," Grant said.

"What?"

"That *your* missing guy—what's his name again?"

"Talbert."

"That Talbert has such a similar work hard/play hard profile. Real estate developer. High net worth. Mr. Life-of-the-Party. How long's he been AWOL?"

"Three days."

"And you think he's just off having some 'me time' too?"

Sophie shook her head. "He missed meetings. Important ones. We sure these guys didn't know each other? Decide to run off to Vegas?"

Grant shook his head. "Nothing points that way, but I'm wondering if there's a connection we've missed."

The roasted earthiness of brewing coffee wafted in from the break room.

The copy machine began to chug in a distant corner.

"What are you thinking?" she asked.

"This is just a stab in the dark, but what sort of trouble might two wealthy, workaholic playboys such as these get themselves into?"

"Drugs."

"Sure, but I didn't get the sense that Seymour was into anything harder than a lot of high-end booze and a little weed. It's not exactly a life-and-death proposition scoring in this city."

"Women."

"Yep."

Sophie smiled, a beautiful thing.

She said, "So you're theorizing our boys were murdered by a serial killer prostitute?"

"Not ready to go that far yet. Just saying let's explore this direction."

"And this hunch is based on ..."

"Nothing at all."

"Glad to see you don't let your training get in the way of your job."

"Can't train instinct, Sophie. You're on Facebook, right?"

"Yeah."

"What do you call it when you ask someone to be your friend? Other than pathetic."

She rolled her eyes. "A friend request."

"Send one to Talbert and Seymour. I'll call my contact at Seymour's office and see if they can log into his account and accept your request. You do the same with Talbert's people."

"You want me to go through and compare their lists of friends."

"Maybe we get lucky and they share some female acquaintances. Facebook is the new street corner." Grant glanced at his watch. "I gotta get outta here."

He stood, grabbed his jacket.

"You're just gonna leave all this to me?"

"Sorry, but I have to drive out to Kirkland. Haven't been in six weeks."

Sophie's eyes softened.

"No problem. I'll get on this."

Chapter 2

Construction paper ornaments hung in chains along the walls of the empty visiting room where Grant sat. Every season, the patients of the acute psychiatric unit who could handle a pair of scissors without hurting themselves or someone else made Christmas decorations for the less stable residents to paint. The results were all over the map. Some were nebulous shapes with smears of color. Others possessed the compulsive detail of a Franciscan altarpiece.

Grant closed the magazine. He'd lost track of how many times he'd perused it in the last year. Judging by the dates on the stack of *National Geographic* in front of him, the tradition was safe for the foreseeable future.

"That article on Russian warplanes must get better and better."

Grant looked up to find an attractive nurse about his age wheeling a man through the doorway.

"A good waiting room magazine ages like fine wine," he said, returning it to the pile. "How is he, Angela?"

"He's been a perfect gentleman."

The man in the wheelchair looked older and gaunter—or maybe Grant just imagined that. His tufts of gray hair could stand a trimming. Grant noticed a bandage peeking out from beneath the nurse's sleeve.

Asked, "He didn't do that, did he?"

"No, we keep his fingernails trimmed now. This is from a patient who had an episode last night."

She parked the wheelchair in front of Grant.

The man's eyes struggled to focus on him, but they had all the control of a pair of marbles.

"Hi, Dad."

Angela smiled apologetically. "He's a little more sedated than usual."

Protocol was to let them know he was coming ahead of time so they could medicate his father. Without the cocktail of depressants, antipsychotics, and muscle relaxers, his father's outbursts were vicious. Even now as his head lolled, padded restraints kept his wrists secured to the wheelchair.

"It's dinnertime," Angela said. "I can bring his tray in and feed him while you visit."

"Is it four o'clock already?"

"Early bird special. Boston clam chowder. They like their routine around here."

"Just bring the food. I'll feed him. Thanks, Angela."

She smiled and left.

Grant pulled his father's chair closer and inspected him. Decades of violent tremors had ruined his physique, the joints and angles of his body gradually becoming more dramatic, muscles ropier, until finally the fifty-nine-year-old man looked like he might have just been unearthed from a tomb.

Grant's greatest fear had once been that he'd never get his father back. But that hope didn't survive the first few years following the crash. Now he feared that contorted body. That his father's mind might be a lucid prisoner inside it.

Angela returned with a rolling tray, and Grant waited until she was gone before examining the food. It was corn chowder. Not clam. And definitely not Boston.

"Well, she was right about the chowder part. Let's see what we have here."

Grant tasted it.

"Not bad. Your turn."

His father's eyes followed the spoon down to the bowl. Grant submerged it and brought it up carefully.

"It's pretty hot."

His father leaned forward slightly to meet it.

"What do you think?"

A dribble escaped. Grant wiped his chin with the napkin.

"They doped you up pretty good this time, huh?"

His father's eyes were vacant and heavy.

It went on like this. The son feeding his father slow spoonfuls. When the bowl was empty, he pushed the tray aside. Through the barred windows of the visiting room, the sky was darkening fast. Grant could scarcely make out the stand of evergreen trees on the southern perimeter of the grounds.

He talked about the weather. How it hadn't flurried yet. About the downtown Christmas traffic which he knew would be waiting for him on the drive home. He talked about work. About Sophie. A movie he'd seen last month. The World Series had come and gone since his last visit, and Grant gave a blow-by-blow of how the St. Louis Cardinals made a record-breaking comeback against the Braves in the Wild Card standings, culminating with their victory over the Rangers in game seven.

"You would've cried," he said.

All the while his father watched him quietly through a glassy-eyed daze that could have been mistaken for listening.

Grant finally stood. Inevitably, in these moments of departure, the stab of loss would run through Grant like a sword. He knew it was coming—every time—but there was no bracing against it. His father had been a great man—kind and brave and a pillar of comfort to his children even through the loss of Grant's mother, his wife, even in the face of his own private hell. Grant couldn't help but to wonder what his life might have become if his father could've looked him in the eyes and spoken his mind, his wisdom? And still the question persisted that had haunted Grant since the night of the accident, that the seven-year-old boy inside of him would never let go—*does something in the shell of you still love me?*

He kissed his old man on the forehead. "Merry Christmas, Pop."

Ten minutes later, he was one of thousands on the congested 520 bridge, slowly making his way home in the early December dark.

Chapter 3

The Space Needle and the cone of Christmas lights at the top made fleeting appearances between the buildings as Grant inched his way home through downtown holiday traffic. First Avenue was a parking lot. As would be the Aurora Bridge that separated him from the kitchen where an expensive bottle of scotch waited—a gift from his Secret Santa at the precinct.

Grant turned the radio off and let his head rest against the window.
Should have cut out of work earlier.
Always ended up staying late at the hospital.
As the traffic crept over Pine, he caught a glimpse of the Macy's star, white-lit and forty feet high. Further up, the Westlake Center Christmas tree stood surrounded by glum shoppers who had been at it for too long—beat down by the eternal drizzle, Christmas Muzak, traffic noise, Salvation Army bells, and pleas for spare change.

Home was Fremont. For Grant it couldn't be anywhere else. In a few minutes he'd be over the Aurora suicide bridge with its high iron fences and winding down the hill into that bright artsy neighborhood on the banks of the Lake Union canal. The rest of the city was a Frankenstein of retro and contemporary architecture. Charming in a schizophrenic way. But Fremont had somehow braced itself against the last thirty years of sprawl. Something timeless about it he just couldn't get enough of.

He found a decent parking spot a block away from his building and jogged through the rain up to the front steps.

His apartment was one of ten units inside a remodeled 1920's townhome. Like so many old houses in the city, it had been endlessly expanded over the last century, and its bloat pressed up against the property lines making narrow alleys of the space between the buildings on either side.

It looks like you're squatting in your own apartment.

Sophie's words on one of her few visits to his Spartan one-bedroom home. *You live like a monk.*

And it was true. If he didn't need it, he didn't own it. There was a loveseat that had come with the place. A floor lamp in the corner. A rug—chic and clearly overqualified for the space—which had been a gift from Sophie in an effort to ease her offended maternal instinct. The only other piece of furniture was the oversized table situated between the kitchen and the dining area. He ate there, worked there, and on rain-soaked Seattle nights like this, he hung his dripping North Face coat on the back of one of its chairs on the way to the kitchen to fix a drink.

Despite his affinity for hoagies and cheap Chinese food, Grant could actually cook and often spent his evenings preparing a meal while he waited for the whiskey-glow to settle in. But he didn't feel particularly culinary tonight. Visits with his father had that effect on him. Instead, he selected a frozen block of lasagna for the microwave, poured the last two fingers from the bottle of scotch he'd gone through in—Jesus, had it only been three days?—and sat down at the table in front of his laptop.

Dinner rotated in the irradiated light behind him.

Seven new e-mails.

All but one were spam.

The legit message was from Sophie.

Subject: Our New Facebook Friends

Guess what? Talbert and Seymour share five "lady friends." Two of them appear to be upstanding members of the community in overlapping social circles. The other three strike me as a bit more mysterious—racy profile pics, aggressive privacy settings which keep their pages suspiciously void of

detailed personal info. It's not much, but it's a start. I think our next step is to gain direct access to the Talbert and Seymour Facebook accounts and see if we can find anything more concrete like direct messages to these women. Hope your afternoon was OK.

Sophie

Grant clicked on one of three links that followed Sophie's e-mail and scanned the first profile. She was right. Not much to go on. There were no posts showing and most of the privacy settings had been enabled, limiting the given data to a name (undoubtedly fake), sex, city, and a lascivious profile pic no more scandalous than what a rowdy college girl might upload after a big weekend.

The next profile lacked the same personal details, and the sole method of contact would be a friend request. Grant felt the familiar exhaustion coming on that preempts a dead-end lead.

He took a larger sip of scotch and opened the last of Sophie's links.

Adrenaline clobbered the beginnings of the evening's buzz.

The profile pic was only a pair of eyes—big and dark and with accentuated lashes so long they seemed almost alien—but the sickening heart-lurch of recognition was unmistakable.

He clicked on the photo album, and with each image, felt the world reorienting itself around this new knowledge.

Grant reached for his jacket on the other side of the table and dug through the pockets until he found his phone. He made a mad swipe across the screen of his contact list. Names ascending in a blur.

He hadn't used the number in almost a year.

Worried he might have deleted it.

Should have deleted it.

There it was.

He dialed.

It rang five times and defaulted to an automated voice mail message he'd heard many times before.

"Hey, Eric, it's Grant. I need to speak with you asap. You can reach me at the number I'm calling from."

He let the phone clatter to the table.

Outside, the rain intensified. It wasn't just misting anymore.

Grant downed the last of the scotch and slid the glass away as the phone illuminated with a new text.

On shift until midnight.

His coat hadn't even begun to dry.

Chapter 4

Grant pulled his black Crown Vic past two idling cabs and parked at the entrance to the Four Seasons.

A bellhop with bad acne scars said, "You leave your car there, it'll be towed."

Grant was already reaching for his wallet. He held it up as he passed the kid, let it fall open, his shield refracting glints of overhead light.

The bellhop called after him, "Sorry about that, sir. It's cool."

Grant shouldered through the revolving doors into the lobby—sleek, modern, and minimally decorated for Christmas with only a handful of evergreen wreaths hanging from the walls. There was stone and wood everywhere, a dynamite contemporary art collection, and a long fireplace near the entrance to the adjoining restaurant and lounge flooding the place with heat.

Grant spotted Eric at the concierge desk. From a distance, he didn't cut the figure of a guy who could stumble you into any type of recreational substance or activity in the city. Looked more like a law student—twenty-four or twenty-five, clean-shaven, hair cropped and pushed forward like classic George Clooney. Tonight, he wore a black single-breasted coat over a Carolina-blue vest and matching tie. Grant waited while Eric patiently gave an older couple directions to the Space Needle, and as they shuffled off, the concierge glanced up from his brochure-laden desk.

Rising, he came around to Grant, fishing a pack of Marlboro Reds out of an inner pocket of his coat.

They stood just inside the entrance overhang, protected from the weather, watching traffic crawl down Union Street.

It was cold.

Rain collected in pools along the sidewalk and streams of it sluiced down the curb toward Elliott Bay.

Eric fired a cigarette.

Grant took out his phone—already had her Facebook profile pic pulled up on the browser, her eyes dark and popping, filling the screen.

He showed it to Eric.

"Know her?"

Eric stared at Grant for a beat.

His looked at the phone.

Nodded.

"I want you to set something up for me for tonight," Grant said.

"That's not going to be possible. She isn't like the others."

"What are you talking about?"

"Just so I'm clear ..." Eric dragged hard on his cigarette. "I'm talking to you as a human being, not a cop, right? I mean, this is for *you*, like before."

"That's right."

"Okay. Good. Look, Gloria isn't your type, man."

Grant smiled. "I didn't realize you'd expanded your services into matchmaking. So now you've acquired some sort of insight into what I want to fuck?"

"She's two thousand for an hour. You telling me you can swing that on your public servant's salary?"

"I didn't come here to see a financial advisor. How do I contact her?"

"Through me."

"Where does she work?"

"Out of her house."

"And where's that?"

"Queen Anne. Look, you don't understand. She's referral-only."

"So refer me."

"She takes care of a handful of clients. A very elite club."

"I'm trying not to get offended here, Eric."

"Haven't I always set you up with excellent companions? All top shelf? All Johnnie Walker? But let's shoot straight. Call it like it is. You're a red- sometimes black-label guy. This woman is Johnnie Walker Blue all the way. Her select group of repeat clients spend between eighty and a hundred thousand dollars a year for her company. She's not a one-shot deal, okay? It's like you're leasing a Lexus. There's a commitment implied."

"I want to see her tonight."

"Grant—"

"Listen to me very, very carefully. I'm going into the bar to have a drink. One drink. Before I'm finished, you're going to come into the bar and tell me that you made it happen. You're also going to buy my drink. If these things don't happen, Eric, I will shut you down."

Eric threw his cigarette into a gutter, exhaling as he shook his head. "When you first came to me, I didn't want to work with a cop. And I told you that. There's an imbalance of power going on right here, and it's not fair."

"Jesus, how old are you? There is no fair. There's only how it is. And *this* is how it is."

"I could—"

Grant stepped hard and fast into the concierge's airspace, pushed him up against the cold brick, smelled the tar and nicotine coming off his breath, his face, his hands.

"You could what, Eric?"

"She's not gonna go for this."

"Then tell her a pretty story. Sell it. I have faith in you. And don't use my real name—first or last."

He slapped Eric on the shoulder and started back toward the hotel entrance.

・・・

Grant slid into an empty chair at the corner of the bar and stared out at the darkness of the bay. Wasn't much to see at eight thirty on a rainy Thursday night—just the reflection of lights from the waterfront buildings.

The lounge was bustling—a small crowd mingled by the floor-to-ceiling windows, everyone clutching small, still-wrapped presents.

Was Christmas just two weeks away?

Last year, he'd dropped two hundred on a world-class single malt. Spent the day plowing through the bottle and watching the Godfather trilogy for the umpteenth time. He'd passed out during the first twenty minutes of *Part III*—no big loss there. Maybe he'd take this Christmas in the same direction. Might be something he could almost look forward to. The start of a tradition. Or maybe he'd put a request in to stay on-call. Get lucky, catch a juicy murder.

Didn't really matter as long as there was a plan.

As long as he didn't let the holiday creep up and catch him off guard. Advanced preparation was the only way somebody with nobody had a prayer of surviving Christmas.

"What can I get you?"

Grant turned his attention to the tall, pretty barkeep. Black vest. Long blond hair pulled back into a ponytail. The clear fresh eyes of someone who'd just come on shift.

"Johnnie Walker Blue, rocks."

"That's seventy-five dollars a shot, just so you know."

"Then make it a double."

Halfway through the glass, he sensed the warmth coming, a pleasant bleariness settling in behind his eyes. But strangely, he didn't feel calmer. Not at all. The only sensation was a shift in the night's energy. The threat of being hurtled in a new, unforeseen direction.

He was down to his last few sips when Eric climbed into the open chair beside him.

"Just texted you her address." As if on cue, Grant felt his phone vibrate. "You have a meet-and-greet in one hour. It's no sure thing. She has to like you. If she doesn't? That's not on me. I told her you were an architect named Michael. You were warned she's expensive. You better pay in full. I gotta tell you … I'm stunned she even went for this."

Grant slugged back the last of his scotch, stepped down off the stool, and grabbed his coat.

Eric said, "If I get complaints, if you burn this bridge for me—"

"Then you'll deal with it, won't you? Thanks for the drink."

Chapter 5

He parked two blocks away on Crockett Street per the directions Eric had texted him and turned off the Crown Vic.

Rain beaded on the windshield, distorting the lights of passing cars. Grant glanced at his phone: 9:25.

The knot in his stomach had been tightening with every mile he'd driven since leaving the Four Seasons, and now it felt taut enough to fray.

He locked his gun in the glove compartment.

Opened the door, stepped out into rain that was cold enough to leave a metallic chill where it touched his skin. Grant raised the hood of his North Face jacket, thrust his hands into the pockets, and started down the sidewalk.

It was an affluent quarter in upper Queen Anne—rows of brownstones interspersed with Victorian mansions. Streetlamps ran along the block, and between the rain falling through their illumination and a haze of mist lingering in the alleyways, the neighborhood assumed the eerie gloom of a nineteenth-century London slum.

At the next block, Grant stopped and stared cattycorner across the intersection at a freestanding brownstone. The building was three stories. It occupied a corner. Evergreen hedges rose almost to the windows of the first-level, and though the curtains were drawn, he could see light around the edges. The second and third floors stood completely dark.

Grant waited for a break in traffic and then jogged across the street, dodging a large puddle several inches deep.

He stopped at the wrought iron fence that encircled the property and leveled his gaze on the front door. The scent of wood smoke was faint in the air.

The number on the small, black mailbox beside the door matched the address he'd been given. He unlatched the gate and pushed his way through, moving along the path of flagstones, and then up the stairs. With each step, he noted a strange sensation, a pressure building in his head, his pace involuntarily quickening, as though he were being pulled toward the building.

Then he was standing under the covered stoop, his pulse at full throttle, trying to catch his breath before he knocked.

A small camera pointed down from just above the door's upper hinge.

This was happening too fast.

His head still hummed from the Johnnie Walker Blue, and he had only the vaguest concept of what he was going to say.

Swallowing the doubt and the fear, he pressed the buzzer.

The muffled thud of footsteps—most likely barefoot—came into range on the other side of the door.

A voice crackled through an intercom under the mailbox.

"Michael, how are you?"

Grant hit the TALK button, leaned in, responded with, "Doing well. Little wet out here."

"Then let's get you out of the cold."

The slide of a chain.

Two deadbolts turning.

Hinges creaking.

A blade of light cut across the stone at Grant's feet as the heavy wood door swung open.

Top-shelf perfume swept over him.

The light was poor.

She wore a purple silk kimono with a pattern of black vines and flowers that curled down the sleeves. Plunging neckline. Her blond hair had been lifted off her neck and shoulders with a pair of black chopsticks.

She stood barefoot in the doorframe, her hand still clutching the knob. Behind her, the darkened room shifted in the firelight.

Grant looked into her face, into her eyes, hoping for some unfamiliar detail, but they all belonged unquestionably to her.

Waves of horror and relief raged through his head.

She tried to shut the door, but he'd anticipated this, the toe of his boot already across the threshold.

"Leave," she said. "Right now."

"I just want to talk to you."

"How dare you."

"Can I come in?"

"You here to arrest me?"

"No."

"How'd you find me?"

"Doesn't matter."

"I want you to leave right now."

"That's not gonna happen."

"What do you want?"

"Just to see you."

"Congratulations. You've seen me. Toodaloo."

"Why do you hate me?"

"I don't hate you." She was still trying to force the door closed.

Grant put his hand up and braced himself against it.

He said, "I didn't know if you were alive or dead. That's the truth. Then I find out you're back in Seattle. You could've reached out to me. You could've made contact."

"And why on earth would I do that?"

"Oh, I don't know. Because I'm your brother?"

"So what?"

"How could you say that?"

"I don't need you sweeping back into my life for a night. Leveling your judgment. Telling me how I'm destroying my life. How I should fix it. How you'll help me—"

"I miss you, Paige. I just want to see you. That's all."

"You're melting my heart."

"Please."

She looked him up and down.

For a moment, there was nothing but the hush of rainfall on the street. The quiet hum of the globe light above their heads. The thunder of Grant's heart slamming inside his chest.

She said finally, "All right, but you leave when I say."

"Yes."

"And you're not here to fix me. You understand that?"

"Yes."

Paige sighed and moved back from the door.

Chapter 6

As Grant stepped inside and pushed the door closed after him, Paige turned and headed up the staircase that launched out of the foyer.

"Where you going?" Grant called after her as the steps creaked under her footfalls.

"To get decent for my brother."

A live jazz album that sounded like Miles Davis played softly from a Bose system in the living room. He caught the scent of essential oils and candles. The air was further laced with incense and the good, spicy smell of cedar burning in the fireplace.

Straight on, a hallway ran parallel to the staircase before feeding into a kitchen. An archway on the left opened into a formal dining room whose rough-hewn table—covered in envelopes and paperwork—appeared to serve the purpose of a desk rather than a place where people actually sat down to eat.

Grant hung his coat on the rack and walked through the archway on his right into the living room. There were candles everywhere. A leather couch against the far wall facing the hearth. A bookcase. Bottles and glassware glimmered in the back corner in the light of the flames—a wet bar. Along the mantle, sprigs of garland peppered with white Christmas lights made for the only decorations in an otherwise seasonally indifferent room.

As orphans, they had gone without, but even in the leanest of times, Paige could always bring a touch of class to whatever miserable living situation they found themselves in. Wild flowers poking out of a glass Coke bottle, the walls of a motel room draped with birthday streamers cut from newspaper; it amazed him what she could do with nothing. Now, he saw the maturation of her gift in the design choices she'd made. The house was old, probably pushing a hundred years, but she had accentuated the early twentieth-century crown molding and sconces with contemporary decor. The living room furniture was upholstered in black leather and sat low to the ground. Beyond the rear doorway, white-lacquered kitchen cabinets gleamed beneath recessed lighting. The only things that hadn't been renovated were the floors and staircase—dark walnut worn smooth from a century of use. Grant wondered what kind of money she made to be able to afford such a place. But that was Paige. Whatever she did, she threw herself into it, and as much as Grant hated the life choices she'd made, damn if he wasn't a little bit impressed.

One of the lower steps creaked. Grant returned to the foyer as Paige appeared around the corner, now dressed in something far warmer and modest—a plaid pajama top and bottom. She had let her hair down, and it fell a few inches past her shoulders. At thirty-six, those once pure and shimmering platinum locks were showing streaks of dishwater.

She'd definitely aged in the five years since their last disastrous rendezvous—a botched intervention attempt in a Motel 6 on the outskirts of Phoenix, last in a fifteen-year string of attempts to save her life. Seemed like ever since Paige had turned sixteen and dropped out of high school, she'd been on a mission to kill herself. Frankly, he was shocked that she hadn't finished the job by now. Despite their estrangement, the threat of that next-of-kin notification phone call was a fear that never left him.

Paige had been so scantily-clad when she first answered the door that Grant hadn't allowed himself to really look at her. Some things, a brother shouldn't see. But now, as she cruised toward him in wool-lined slippers into the firelight, it struck him how thin she was. Borderline emaciation. The long-sleeved pajama top seemed to swallow her, and her face tapered from her cheekbones down toward her chin at angles so sharp they didn't seem natural—the shape of her skull shining through.

Using for sure.

"Place is incredible," Grant said.

"The rent certainly is."

It occurred to him that he'd missed his chance to inspect her arms for needle-marks when she'd been wearing the short-sleeved kimono.

Bad detective.

"How long you been in town?" he asked.

"A year."

"You're kidding me."

"But I've only been in this place two months."

Grant stepped toward the small fireplace and held his hands to the heat.

"Want a drink?" she asked.

"Love one."

She padded over to the wet bar, moving like someone with barely the strength to stand—a nursing home shuffle.

"Still a scotch man?"

"For life."

He watched her reach for a bottle of Macallan. The lowlight stopped him from determining the age.

"Neat? Rocks?" she asked.

"What year?"

"Twenty-one."

"Jesus. Then neat."

She made a generous pour. Brought it over. Out of habit, he lifted the glass and inhaled. It was a gorgeous nose but flattened by the occasion.

"Seriously," she said. "How'd you find me?"

"Dumb luck."

"Facebook?"

"Yep."

"My profile is only a pair of eyes."

"But they're your eyes."

Grant sipped the whiskey.

Miles Davis was blistering through a trumpet solo.

The fire popping.

He looked down at his sister, a good six inches shorter than he was.

No idea what to say.

He raised his glass. "Some of the best I've had."

Paige just stared at him and nodded.

Grant looked around the room as if it were his first time seeing it. "No tree?"

She shook her head. "Think I waited too long. You have to do that kind of stuff early in the season. Before you lose the motivation."

It was Grant's turn to nod.

"This is weird," she said

"I know."

Another sip. His cheeks flushing.

"Do you visit Dad?" she asked.

"Not enough. Every few weeks."

"I went once when I first moved back from Phoenix. That's all I could bear. You think I'd be used to seeing him like that by now."

"I was just there this afternoon. They had Christmas ornaments up. Slit your wrists depressing."

He flinched inside. Shouldn't have put it that way.

Grant could feel the scotch already beginning to soften his knees. He moved toward the couch. A mattress and blanket had been shoved underneath it. Did she fuck her clients down here by the fireside? Right on this floor where he was standing? He pushed the thought away.

"I want you to know that I thought about contacting you," Paige said as he lowered himself onto the cushion.

"Wish you had."

Grant sipped his drink and watched the fire.

Through the window at his back, he could hear the rain falling on the hedges.

"I do have one favor to ask," Grant said.

She grimaced.

"Relax, it's not a big deal. I just haven't eaten since lunch and this whiskey is going to my head in a hurry."

"You want me to make you something?"

"How about I make *us* something. Are you hungry?"

She smiled, and for a split second, it was like a window into the Paige of old. A break in the armor. "You mean like your world famous grilled cheese?"

"I have a confession to make. It's not actually world famous."

Chapter 7

The square of butter sizzled as Grant guided it around the pan with a wooden spatula. Paige sat on a barstool at the kitchen island, skillets and copper sauce pans of every size dangling above her head from a hanging pot rack.

"Mild cheddar or Jack?" Grant asked.

"You don't remember?"

"American cheese it is."

Grant opened the door to the fridge. Not exactly a wellspring of food—just a half-empty jug of skim milk two weeks past expiration, the usual condiments, three cardboard pizza boxes, a colony of leftover Chinese cartons, and yes, a stack of plastic-wrapped slices.

He returned to the stove with the mayo and Kraft Singles, trying but failing to remember the last time he'd made a grilled cheese sandwich, even for himself. Wondered if that had been a subconscious thing. This had once been their meal of choice, if not necessity. Just the smell of browning butter conjured up that year they'd fled foster care and lived on their own in a drafty single-wide on the outskirts of Tacoma. Grant fifteen, Paige thirteen. They'd lasted nine months before Social Services caught up with them.

Cold, broke, always hungry, yet it surpassed, in every way, living with strangers.

Grant eased the sandwiches onto the skillet and left them to sizzle.

Sat across from Paige at the island.

Under the brighter recessed lighting in the kitchen, she looked even worse. What he'd mistaken for her good complexion was foundation. Her skin was sallow, eyes bloodshot and underscored with black bags that the concealer couldn't quite conceal. The way she sat on her hands made him wonder if it was to hide their trembling.

"I'm sorry I just showed up," Grant said.

"You mean that?"

"Yeah."

She reached across the table and touched his hand.

"I just didn't know if you'd see me again," Grant said. "Considering how we left it last time."

He pulled away and slid off the stool, headed back to the stove.

"I could never make them taste the way yours did," Paige said as he moved the sandwiches onto plates.

"You probably missed the most important step."

"Which one's that?"

"You have to add a new pat of butter to the skillet when you're halfway done. So each side gets the love."

"Equal opportunity buttering—I like it."

Grant watched the new square melt. He lifted the skillet, let the butter skate across the surface for a few seconds before flipping the cold sides of the sandwiches onto the heat.

"So what do you think, big bro? Your sister, the whore. That's a new one, right?"

Grant stared down into the skillet.

She'd always liked to fuck with him, but this wasn't even fair.

"You're talking about someone I love," he said, pressing the spatula into the sandwiches.

They sizzled.

Grant finally lifted the sandwiches onto the plates and carried them over to the island.

"Bon appétit."

He was hungrier than he'd realized, and drunker too. In between bites, he caught bursts of electric clarity—he was actually sitting in Paige's kitchen, sharing a meal with her.

As she lifted the sandwich to her mouth, the sleeves tugged back from her wrists. He glimpsed the scars from a past suicide attempt, but thankfully, no needle sores.

"How's the sandwich?"

Through a mouthful: "Unbelievable."

A full minute passed.

Neither of them spoke but it wasn't as uncomfortable as before.

Jazz slunk in from the living room.

Grant watched as Paige took tiny bites. Just the effort of eating seemed to pain her.

She said, "I just assumed you were still with the PD, but are you?"

"I am."

"And how's that going?"

"Fine."

"Yeah? Some interesting cases?"

"Always."

"So you like what you do."

"I love it. Do you?"

"Do I love what you do?"

"You know what I mean."

"I'm making fat bank, Grant."

"So I hear."

"What's that supposed to mean?"

"I had to threaten Eric to get a referral."

"Not cool."

"He made it sound like you didn't see guys like me."

"Like you?"

"Low net-worth individuals."

"Wait. You're upset I won't just fuck anyone who slides me a couple of hundreds?"

She had a point there.

"How about a tour of the place?" Grant asked. "Love to see what you've done with the upstairs."

Her eyes went wide; her breathing accelerated.

"No."

"Why?"

"No." She practically yelled it the second time, leaning toward him across the island, her eyes narrowing, teeth grinding together, the ugly monstrous addict rearing its head.

"Fine. Sorry I asked."

Grant got up and walked over to the Bose—Miles Davis noodling away on the trumpet.

"Bitches Brew? Not his most popular but as good as anything he ever did. I love this part." He turned the volume up a few decibels. "Where's your bathroom?"

Paige pointed to the door at the end of the kitchen.

Chapter 8

Grant sat down on the edge of the bathtub.

Fished the phone out of his pocket and scrolled through the contact list. *Don McFee.*

One of the first friends Grant had made after leaving the academy. One of the few who'd stuck around during those dark days after Paige disappeared in Phoenix and he'd been hell-bent on death by escorts and scotch.

Don answered on the fifth ring, a sleep-drawl in his voice.

"I wake you?" Grant asked, speaking low into the phone.

"It's all right."

"I'm going to owe you huge for this one."

"Then I guess I'll keep the tab running."

"I'm at my sister's place in Queen Anne. Twenty-two Crockett Street. It's not far from your house."

"You're with Paige?"

"Long story. She's not looking so hot right now. I've never seen her so thin. She's wasting away."

"Grant, we've been through this. You can't fix her."

"This isn't like the other times. She looks like a chemo patient."

"Let me come pick you up. We'll get some coffee and talk about it."

"I'm not leaving my little sister like this."

"You want me to show up uninvited at ten o'clock so I can tell her she's an addict? I love you, man, but that road leads nowhere. You want to do another intervention, fine, but let's do it the right way."

"I'm not asking you as a counselor."

"Is her life in imminent danger?"

"No."

"Then as your friend, I'm telling you this isn't what she needs. An ambush will only work against you."

"Did I mention she's a prostitute? I haven't seen her in five years, and now she's fucking guys for cash."

"Christ. I'm sorry."

"Don't make me do this on my own, Don."

There was a long pause.

A blizzard of trumpet notes escalated into a wail that sustained itself for so long Grant suddenly felt the need for a deep breath.

"Have you been drinking tonight, Grant?"

"Little bit."

"Let me come get you."

"Don't worry about it. Sorry to wake you."

Grant ended the call.

He needed a new plan.

The light above the sink flickered several times.

Went out.

Miles Davis gone silent.

Grant struggled onto his feet.

"Paige?"

The shower cut on, the cramped little bathroom filling with the noise of moving water as the pitch-black disorientation set in.

Where was the door again?

He stumbled forward into a towel rack as the toilet flushed of its own volition.

In a span of seconds, he lost all perception of space.

Need to get out of here.

He moved in another direction and ran into the sink.

The faucet turned on.

It felt like the room was closing in on him, the walls contracting, the ceiling pressing down, a completely illogical panic building, accompanied by a shortness of breath.

And then the lights kicked on.

He was staring at himself in the mirror and his chest was heaving and all that running water had silenced itself so quickly he wondered if he'd imagined the noise.

Chapter 9

Paige was at the sink when Grant emerged.

He walked over and grabbed a towel off the door to the Sub-Zero fridge.

"You lose power out here too?" Grant asked.

"Yeah. Happens occasionally. Old house, comes with the territory I guess."

"You should get that checked. You'd be surprised how many old houses in the city burn down every month because the wiring is for shit."

The left sink brimmed with dishes that had just begun to smell.

They fell into a familiar pattern—Paige washing, Grant drying.

Steam peeled off the surface of the murky dishwater and fogged the window behind the sink.

It felt good to have his hands doing something, and the strangeness he'd encountered in the bathroom was fading away like the memory of a dream.

As his sister handed him a plate, he said, "Can I be honest with you?"

"I hope so."

"I'm worried about you."

"You should have that put on a T-shirt."

"You don't look well, Paige."

"Ouch." She handed him the cast iron skillet. "Oil this for me."

Grant grabbed a bottle of olive oil from the windowsill and sprinkled a few drops across the surface. Then he tore off a paper towel and began to massage it into the iron.

"I swear I didn't come over to fix things, but I can't ignore it either."

Paige let a plate slide into the dishwater and turned to him.

"And here I was just beginning to think that maybe this was the start of something different. Good job. You really took my guard down."

"You look terrible, Paige. You're pale, thin, weak. You can barely walk."

"I'm tired."

"Are you eating?"

"Did you just *see* me eat?"

"Then what's going on?"

Paige braced herself against the counter and stared at the wall. Grant recognized that stony expression. Total system failure. Whenever Paige felt cornered, she went on lockdown, and there was no getting back in.

The chime of the doorbell cut through the jazz, snapping Paige back into the moment.

She went over to the Bose, muted the speakers, and headed up the hallway into the foyer.

Grant hung back.

A client dropping by?

Paige said, "Can I help you?"

A man's voice crackled over the intercom. "I'm looking for Grant Moreton."

"Just a minute."

Paige turned and stared down the corridor. Even in the lowlight, he could see the rage in her eyes.

"Someone's here for you," she said.

He started down the hall.

"How would anyone know you're here?"

Grant passed the staircase and moved into the foyer.

"No idea."

Keep digging that grave.

"Is this another cop?" she asked.

"Of course not."

Grant slid the chains out of their guards and unlocked the multiple deadbolts.

"Don't just open it for him," Paige said, but he was already turning the doorknob.

Don McFee stood on the front porch, rain pouring behind him, pooling in the street, in the small square of grass that constituted the front yard.

The man's face was half-shadowed under the hood of his Barbour coat, the jacket's oiled surface beaded with rainwater.

"This is a terrible idea," Don muttered under his breath as Grant let him in.

Paige said, "Who's this?"

"Don McFee," Don said, extending his hand. "You must be Paige."

"What's going on, Grant?"

Grant closed the door after them.

"Don is a friend of mine."

Paige glared at Don.

His coat dripped on the hardwood floor.

"You better be here to take Grant home."

Don looked at Grant and then at Paige. His head was shaved. Kind but intense eyes peered out from behind a pair of frameless lenses. He wore a calming presence that Grant could never reduce to its components or attribute to any particular quality. The guy just oozed Zen.

Don said, "I wonder if I might be of some help to you first?"

"Excuse me?"

Don looked her up and down. "I've been a substance abuse counselor for sixteen years."

"Oh my God."

"Please just hear me—"

"And what? Grant called you and told you I was using?" She looked at Grant. "Is that what you did? While you were in the bathroom?"

"Are you using, Paige?" Don asked.

"Get the fuck out of my house both of you."

Grant said, "Paige, just talk to—"

She lunged forward, and with both hands, shoved Grant back against the door.

"I can't believe I trusted you."

"He can help. He's helped me."

"Did you hear me ask for help?"

"Paige—"

"Did you?"

"Your brother's concerned," Don said. "And I have to agree with him. You don't look well."

"Get out of my house."

"Nobody's leaving," Grant said.

Paige turned away from them and moved quickly into the living room, stopping at an end table that rested against the couch.

She lifted a cordless phone off its base.

"Really want to give the cops your address?" Grant said.

Paige held the phone against her chest and shut her eyes.

When she opened them again, her body language had relaxed, as if some of the fight was flooding out of her.

She looked at Grant. "I appreciate your concern, okay? But there is nothing wrong with me, and I am asking both of you to please leave."

Don stepped in. "Paige, I don't think I need to tell you that you're underweight, your complexion is unhealthy, and your hair is thin. My job isn't to scare you, but your body can't handle much more than it's already been put through."

"I've been clean for three years."

Don moved slowly into the living room. "All the more reason to find out what's going on. Wouldn't you at least agree that your physical appearance is a cause for alarm?"

Paige stared at the floor, and for the first time since walking into this house, Grant sensed a change in her. It didn't hold the power of an outright admission, but at least she wasn't swinging back, trying to tear his throat out.

"How do you feel right in this moment, Paige?" Don asked.

She collapsed onto the couch. Let out a long sigh.

"Honestly? I'm tired," she said. "I'm weak all the time." Grant thought he registered emotion—coiled and charged—bleeding into her voice. "Even when I was strung out it never felt this bad."

Grant hung back while Don continued toward her with the greatest care—as if approaching a wounded animal. Don unzipped his jacket and draped it over the back of a chair. He settled down on the couch beside Paige.

"Have you been to see a doctor?" he asked.

She shook her head.

"Are you afraid to go?"

Paige had been staring at her hands. Now she looked up at the ceiling. "No."

"Don't you think it would help you to find out what the problem is?"

"It doesn't matter. A doctor's not what I need."

"Why not?"

"Because I'm not sick the way you think I am."

Grant exchanged a glance with Don, and then said, "Paige, if you say you're clean then I believe you."

"I'm not talking about drugs."

"Then I'm lost," Don said. "What's making you sick?"

She shook her head.

When it was clear she wasn't going to answer, Don said, "Paige, how about we just try the hospital? You don't have to tell them anything. Just let them examine you. Take your vitals."

Paige sighed. "I can't."

"You can. I'm parked right around the block. All you have to do is stand up and walk out that front door. Grant and I will do the rest."

Paige finally looked up, tears shining in the firelight.

Her eyes darted to the door. "It's not that easy."

"I know it's diff—"

"You don't know. You have no idea."

"Then tell us," Grant said.

Her eyes flicked from Don to Grant and back. "I can't leave the house."

"Why?"

"I get sick if I try."

"You look pretty sick right now."

"This is nothing compared to what happens if I go out that door."

"Have you ever had a panic attack, Paige?"

"Yes. That's not what this is."

"Then what is it?"

"You won't believe me."

"Paige." Don touched her shoulder. "There is no judgment in this room."

"I'm not worried about you judging me. I'm worried about you committing me."

Grant said, "Whatever it is, I already believe you."

She looked at Grant. "Don't say that if you don't mean it."

"I mean it."

"Something's keeping me here."

"*Physically* keeping you from leaving?" Grant asked.

She went silent, but her eyes were pleading, desperate. Grant came over and knelt on the floor beside her.

He said quietly, "Paige, is there something you can't tell us?"

Those words ripped her apart.

She leaned over into the cushion, and everything seemed to release at once in a rush of tears.

Grant pushed a few loose strands of hair behind her ear.

"What is it, Paigy?" he whispered. "What's doing this to you? Is it a client?"

She shook her head. "It's in my bedroom upstairs. Under the bed."

"What is?"

"I don't know. Something that shouldn't be."

Grant noted a sickening chill plunge down his spine, prompted by a realization he'd been fighting against all his life: his sister was crazy.

He glanced down at the mattress poking out from underneath the couch.

"You've been sleeping down here, haven't you?"

"Yes."

"Because you're afraid to go upstairs."

She nodded into the couch.

Grant looked up at his friend.

Don said, "Paige, I just want to make sure I understand exactly what you're saying. Something under your bed is keeping you from leaving the house."

"Yes."

"And you don't know what it is?"

She shook her head.

"Are you talking about a flesh-and-blood person?" Grant asked.

"I told you. I don't know."

Don said, "Sometimes, we sink down to these bad places in our lives and we lose the ability to distinguish between what's real and what's—"

"I know how fucked-up this sounds, okay?"

"Do you want my help, Paige?"

"That's the only reason you're still in my house."

Don said, "Then come with me."

"Where?"

"Upstairs."

"No."

"We're going to walk into your bedroom—"

"I can't—"

"—and I'm going to show you there's nothing in there that has an ounce of power over you. Then we're going to do whatever it takes to get you better."

Paige sat up. She was trembling. "You don't understand—we can't go in there together."

"Then I'll go by myself."

Paige struggled to her feet. She said, "You don't have my permission to go upstairs," but the edge in her voice was ebbing.

Don said, "I fully respect how real this feels to you. But I'm going to go up there, have a look, come back down, and tell you that everything's okay. That there's nothing in your room. That, as real as this may feel, it's in your mind."

All the fight was leaving her.

She looked scattered and helpless.

Don crossed the living room, which had fallen into near-darkness now that the fire was dying.

He stopped at the bottom of the staircase.

"Which room, Paige?"

"Please don't."

"Which room?"

"Turn right at the top of the stairs, round the corner, and go down to the end of the hall. My bedroom is the door at the end."

"Grant, would you come with me?"

Grant followed Don.

The staircase lifted out of the foyer into darkness.

"She's cracked," Grant whispered as they climbed.

Each step creaked like the hull of an old ship.

"She doesn't look well, and this paranoid delusion about something keeping her in the house is disturbing."

"So what do I do?"

"Consider an involuntary commitment."

"Seriously?"

"I can help you with the paperwork."

"Great. Maybe she can room with Dad."

The meager light that warmed the foyer fell away behind them.

They climbed the last few steps into complete darkness and stopped, waiting for their eyes to adjust.

Grant looked over to where Don stood, but could make out nothing of his shape.

"Let's find a light switch," Don said.

Grant heard him shuffle over to the wall and begin feeling his way along it. Grant followed suit, groping across wallpaper but his fingers only grazed a few picture frames. He continued down the hall and then around a corner, both hands guiding him along like a caver without a light. At last, he barked his shin against the leg of a table, rattling its contents.

"You okay?" Don called from the other side.

"Yeah."

Grant's fingers moved across the surface of the table until they came to what felt like the base of a lamp.

He followed it up, found the switch.

Weak yellow light filled the hallway, barely enough to reach the far end.

The ceiling was high and the walls so close together it almost looked like an optical illusion. Grant was struck with a fleeting imbalance, like standing in a funhouse, the proportions all wrong.

The carpeting was thick, burgundy, and old.

The wallpaper peeled in places, the Plaster of Paris underneath far more appealing than the maudlin floral print. Along the opposite wall, a cast-iron radiator belched out waves of heat that did little against the chill. Grant had fumbled down the hallway farther than he realized. The bedroom door loomed straight ahead, its thick frame detailed with scrollwork that matched the wainscoting.

It sounded like Paige had begun to cry down on the first floor.

Johnny Cash punctuated the moment with a muffled rendition of "Ring of Fire."

Grant's heart jolted.

He turned to find Don staring down at the wailing cell phone in his hand.

"It's just Rachel," Don said.

"I think Paige is crying. I'm going to head back down."

"Sounds good. Let me deal with this call, and then I'll handle things up here."

Grant walked quickly back toward the staircase, secretly glad to be leaving that drafty hallway.

Chapter 10

Paige was curled up on the couch, and as soon as she saw him, she turned away and wiped the mascara stains from her cheeks.

Grant sat down on the hardwood floor at eye level with his sister.

Laid his hand carefully on her shoulder.

"I don't know how I got to this point," she said. "You ever feel that way?"

"Absolutely. I've had my share of spinouts. All that matters is you're moving forward. Things are going to get better."

"I sound like a crazy person."

"You should've seen me a few years back."

She wiped her cheeks again and rolled over to face him.

"But did you ever feel like you didn't know what was real?"

He shook his head.

"It sucks."

"You and I have never been crybabies about anything, but we haven't exactly lived the nuclear family dream."

"So?"

"So cut yourself a little slack, all right?"

"I don't want to be crazy."

In their entire lives, Grant couldn't think of anything his sister had said to him—even during her drugged-out ravings—that hit him so hard. It was a killshot, and he could feel his heart breaking as she stared at him. Yet another moment of Paige in agony, and not a damn thing he could do to make it better.

"Do you trust me?" he asked.

"I'm trying."

"Will you let me help you get help?"

For a long time, she didn't say anything. Just stared at him as her eyes glistened with a reinforcement of tears.

At last she said, "I will, Grant."

He leaned in, kissed her cheek.

The room had grown dark and cold.

All that remained of the fire was a single log with glowing ember veins.

"Is there more wood?" he asked.

"There's a wrap in the pantry."

Grant went to the kitchen and dug three logs out of the bundle. He carried them into the living room and dragged away the screen. The bed of coals put out the faintest purple glow.

He arranged the logs on the grate, blew the embers back to life.

The new wood caught easily.

Grant turned, letting the heat lap at his back as he watched the firelight play across Paige's face. She looked beyond tired. Like she could sleep for months.

What was taking Don so long? Had he found drugs?

"Remember when we squatted in that abandoned house for a few weeks?" he said. "No electricity. Just a fireplace."

"Yeah. We burned wooden crates that you found behind a grocery store."

"Things have been worse than this, Paige."

"But I don't look back on that and call it a low point."

"Seriously?"

"Those were the moments when I knew we'd be okay. Life could get shitty but we were in it together."

"We're in *this* together too."

Grant heard footsteps on the second floor.

Finally—Don on his way down.

The footfalls accelerated.

Was he running?

Grant instinctively looked up at the ceiling as if he could see through it.

Something crashed to the floor.

A door closed hard enough to shake the walls.

Grant looked at Paige.

She'd sat up, arms crossed over her chest and her face screwed up like she was going to vomit.

"Stay here," he said.

"Don't go up there. Don't leave me."

"I'll be right back."

Grant crossed to the foot of the stairs and jogged up as his sister called after him.

At the top, he rounded the corner.

Stopped.

"Don? Everything okay?"

The table had been knocked over and the lamp lay on its side, bulb still intact, casting an uneasy triangle of light across the ancient carpeting.

Stepping over the debris, he moved quickly down the hall, the darkness growing as he strayed from the lamp.

The door to Paige's bedroom was still closed.

He stopped in front of it.

Tried the knob.

It wouldn't turn.

He pounded on the door.

"Don? You okay?"

Nothing.

Grant reared back, on the brink of digging his shoulder into the door, when the bright chinkle of breaking glass stopped him.

The sound had come from another hallway.

He rushed through in near-darkness, and only as he approached a door at the end did he notice the faintest thread of light along the bottom of its frame.

He burst through into a sparse bedroom. The duvet was pristine and the air musty and redolent of a rarely-used guestroom.

"Don?"

A splash of light spilled onto the hardwood floor through a cracked door in the far wall.

Four steps and he was standing in front of it.

Grant pushed the door open all the way with the tip of his boot.

The mirror was shattered, a web of fractures expanding out from the center.

Shards of crimson glass lay in the sink.

Don sat on the floor facing the doorway, his legs spread out, back against the clawfoot bathtub.

He was staring at Grant and holding a piece of the mirror to his own throat.

"Don? What are you doing?"

Don's eyes looked so strange—roiling with an incomprehensible intensity.

"Don."

Don spoke softly, "All your life you believe certain things about the world, only to learn how wrong you were."

"You went into Paige's room?"

Don nodded slowly. "I looked under the bed." He shut his eyes fiercely for a second and tears slipped down the sides of his face. "And now it's in my head, Grant."

"What are you talking about?"

"I can feel it pushing me to … do things."

"What things?"

Don shook his head.

"Put that piece of glass down," Grant said.

"You don't understand."

"I know who you are, Don. I know your kindness. Your strength. I know that you couldn't walk into a room, see something, and decide to hurt yourself. You're stronger than this."

"You believe that, Grant? Really?"

"With all my heart."

"You don't know anything. Don't ever go in there."

Grant edged toward him. "Don—"

"Promise me."

"I promise. Now give me the—"

Tension flashed across Don's face—a burst of sudden resolve—and then he pulled the glass through his neck.

It was like a velvet curtain falling out of his throat, streams and tributaries branching down his plaid button-up and flooding out onto the checkerboard tile.

"No!"

Grant rushed toward him and ripped the triangle of glass out of Don's hand. He knelt beside him and held his palm across his friend's throat, trying to stem the tide, but the cut was too deep, too wide, and smiling from ear to ear.

Don's eyes were still open but settling more and more with every passing second into a permanent vacancy. His chest barely rising and falling.

"Oh God, Don. Oh, God."

The man's right leg twitched.

The quantity of blood inching toward Grant was tremendous.

Don's jaw worked up and down, but no sound issued except for a soft gurgle in his windpipe.

The change in Don's eyes was both infinitesimal and epic.

His body sagged to the side, his chest fell, and never rose again.

"Don? Don?"

There was so much blood, and he was gone.

Grant sat down on the toilet.

He put his head in his hands and tried to think, but there was too much competition—too many questions, too much fear and sadness, and a part of him still not fully committed to believing that any of this was actually happening.

Grant shut his eyes.

Walking blindly into murder scenes was a part of his job description, and emotional survival depended upon his ability to detach, no matter how horrific the carnage.

But there was no detaching from this. From what his friend had just done to himself.

Grant stood, and as he left the bathroom, he heard Paige calling up to him from the first floor.

He walked out into the dark hallway, his boots tracking blood across the floor.

Paige's bedroom door was still closed. Not even a scintilla of light sneaking out from beneath it. Nothing to suggest that a man had just killed himself after leaving that room.

There's something deeply wrong with this brownstone. On some level, he'd known it the moment he set foot inside, but the knowledge was crushing him now, a wellspring of fear expanding inside of him accompanied by a burning, physical need to leave this place, to get outside. Now.

Grant walked past Paige's room without breaking stride, turned the corner, descended the stairs.

"Where's your friend?" Paige asked as he emerged from the bottom of the staircase into the living room. She was still sitting on the couch, her legs drawn into her chest, arms wrapped around her knees.

"We're leaving," he said.

"What happened?"

"Get your stuff."

"Where's Don?"

"Upstairs."

"What happ— Oh my God, your hands."

He'd been in too much of a state of shock to notice—they were covered in blood.

"I'll tell you in the car."

Paige didn't move.

He pulled his North Face off the coat rack and shot his arms through the sleeves.

"Paige. Get up. We're leaving."

"What happened to your friend?"

"It doesn't—"

"Is he dead?"

Grant hesitated, gave a short nod, tears misting in the corners of his eyes. Paige brought her hand to her mouth.

"We're not staying here," Grant said.

"I can't leave."

Grant crossed to where she sat and grabbed her arm, jerking her up from the couch onto her feet and propelling her through the living room toward the front door.

"Stop! You don't understand!"

"You're right. I don't understand the mindfuck I just witnessed upstairs."

Grant opened the door and pushed her out onto the front porch.

The temperature had dropped and the steady pinpricks of rain had given way to a rare Seattle torrential.

Paige threw her weight into him, trying to claw her way back inside.

"I can't be out here!" she screamed.

Grant pulled the door shut and held Paige so tightly by her arms that his knuckles blanched.

"We're going to walk to my car, get inside, and drive away from this house. While we're doing that, I'm going to call the station and tell them there's a dead man in your bathroom. And do you know what *you're* going to do while all that's happening?"

The way she stared at him, her eyes glazing, made him wonder if she was comprehending a word.

He went on, "You're going to sit there quietly and *let me handle this.*"

Paige dropped her head.

"All right," she said.

Grant let go of her and started down the steps.

Halfway to the bottom, he heard a shuffle behind him, swung around to see Paige dashing toward the front door.

He went after her.

Paige grabbed the doorknob as he hooked his arm around her waist.

She bucked against him, jutting the back of her head into his face.

His nose and eyes burned and he tasted blood on the back of his tongue.

For a second he stood there dazed, arm encircling her midsection as she tried to wrench herself loose. He bent down, hoisted her up and over his shoulder.

She felt impossibly light.

"Stop!" she screamed, pounding her fists against his back.

Grant carried her down the steps and onto the hexagonal flagstones that comprised the walkway.

With each step, Paige's thrashing became more violent.

A throb of pain bubbled up behind his eyes, a pressure more intense than the deepest water he'd ever experienced.

Grant stopped, the pain so sudden and vibrant it wiped his focus.

He was completely disoriented, a dull mud unfolding over his brain.

He looked around, standing in the rain with Paige's now-limp body slung over his shoulder.

Grant took another step forward.

The pressure in his head intensified, like someone turning a crank.

A core of white-hot agony blooming in his gut.

He managed one more step before his knees buckled and hit concrete, Paige's body thudding to the ground in front of him.

Everything buzzed, the world electrified.

He wanted to crack his head open right there on the flagstone, let the pain spill out and wash away in the rain.

Grant threw up on the stone—a violent, spewing rope of alcoholic bile—and his forehead came to rest on the wet rock. He'd let one of the beat cops tase him as a result of a bet gone wrong—this was worse by a factor of five.

Was this what Don had felt?

A whisper, barely audible, found its way to him through the downpour.

He lifted his head, saw Paige on her side, staring at him through wild, desperate eyes, her face inexplicably thinner, degenerating right in front of him as she convulsed.

"What?" he groaned.

"Get us ... inside."

"I can't."

"It's gonna kill us."

Her words cut through the gauze that packed his head and sparked a moment of blinding clarity.

We're going to die out here.

Grant struggled up, half-standing, hands braced on his knees.

It felt like his brain was peeling away from the walls of his skull.

"Can you stand?" he asked.

No answer.

Grant pushed Paige onto her back and grabbed her wrists.

Her eyes threatening to roll up into her head.

"Push with your feet," he groaned.

They made it six inches on the first pull, Grant lunging back toward the steps while Paige kicked at the slick stones.

Even less the second.

It went on like this, their progress measured in inches, Grant pausing between each effort to catch his breath and wince through the pain.

The rain added what felt like pounds to her body. He could hear the thin fabric of her pajama bottoms tearing as her legs slid across the concrete.

By the time he reached the first step, their clothes were soaked and hanging like lead drapes.

"Almost there, Paige."

He dragged her up the steps.

The last pull sent him sprawling back onto the porch, where he lay for a minute, staring up at the light, trying to catch his breath.

"Paige, you okay?"

She coughed and rolled over to face him.

"Better," she said.

The pain in Grant's head had relented, but the fog lingered. It suddenly occurred to him that he'd just dragged what looked like a dead body across the front yard in a crowded neighborhood at God knows what time of night. The thought was enough to give him the final shock of adrenaline he needed to throw Paige's shivering body over his shoulder again and haul her inside.

Grant shut the door behind them and stumbled into the living room.

Fell to his knees, lay Paige on the warm hardwood in front of the fire.

He sprawled across the floor beside her.

They lay shivering in a silence broken only by the crackling logs and the ticking of rain against the windowglass.

In the stillness, Grant noticed the same pressure in his head that he'd felt at the beginning of the evening as he walked up the steps to Paige's front door—a stuffy tightness, like sitting in the canned atmosphere of a fuselage at cruising altitude. He held his nose and tried to pop his ears but nothing happened.

Paige said, "I wanted so bad to be crazy."

"I thought you were."

"I know."

"When I walked in here tonight it looked like you hadn't left this house in a long time."

Grant's pulse rate was dropping out of the red.

"Not in two weeks."

"Is that when this started?"

"No, it started a month ago, every day intensifying until I couldn't even go beyond the front steps. Until I was confined to my house like a prisoner. You went in my room, didn't you?"

"No."

"Don't lie to me, Grant."

"I swear."

"Then why is it affecting you?"

"You tell me."

"I don't know. Don's really dead?"

"He is."

"How?"

"He broke the mirror in the guest bathroom and used it to cut his throat. He was a great man, Paige." Grant could feel the emotion pressing in. "A great friend. Oh God, his wife." A tidal wave of grief was bearing down, but he pushed it back.

Not the time. Need to think.

Grant shuffled closer to the fire. His cold, drenched clothing still clung to him, but waves of heat were washing over his face.

"I woke up one night," Paige said, her voice barely more than a whisper, "and it was just there."

"What was?"

"A presence."

"In your room?"

"Under the bed. Remember tag? How when you were *it* you'd sneak up on me while I was hiding? Get real close. Scare the shit out of me."

"Sure."

"Whenever you did that, a split second before you grabbed me, I'd get this premonition that you were there. That's what it feels like everywhere I go in this house." She was becoming emotional again. "Like something is right behind me all the time. I swear I can almost feel its breath on the back of my neck. I dream about it constantly."

"You're certain this isn't just in your mind?"

"Are *you* imagining this? Was Don?"

"And you sleep down here now?"

"When I'm able to sleep at all. Whatever it is, it's made my bedroom home."

"You've never seen it?"

"No."

"And all those leftovers in your fridge?"

"I've been living off delivery for two week. I'd have starved to death if I didn't run a cash business."

"How often do you try to leave?"

"I test it every day."

"And the same thing always happens?"

"Yeah. In the beginning, I could make it to the street. Tonight, the pain started the moment I stepped out on the porch."

"Jesus."

"It's worse than that, Grant."

"This seems pretty bad all by itself."

"I don't know what it is, but I know what it wants."

"What's that?"

"People. My clients. And the longer I hold out, the sicker I get."

"Are you telling me there's more than one dead man upstairs?"

"I don't know what happens to them." Paige rolled over and faced him. "I tried not to. Tried to resist. But the longer I did, the sicker I got. I was *dying*."

"I don't understand."

"I take a client upstairs. While we're doing our thing, I black out. When I wake up, they're gone. I have no idea what it does with them."

"How many men have you taken up there?" Grant asked.

"Two."

Two.

"But it wants another one. It wants it now. You're the first appointment I took in three days, and I took it with no referral because I'm desperate and couldn't reach any of my core clients. I didn't want to, but this thing … it's killing me."

Are these Sophie's and my missing men?

Seymour and Talbert?

The cases that brought me to Paige's doorstep in the first place?

Maybe better to sit on that piece of news for the time being.

Grant forced himself to sit up. "I should make some calls."

"No."

"No?"

"Do you understand what's happening here?" she asked.

"No."

"So what makes you think someone else will? You'll just get them, or us, or everyone killed."

Paige struggled to her feet.

"Where are you going?" Grant asked.

"My little black book."

Grant managed to stand. He reached into his inner pocket, took out his phone.

"Are you crazy?" Paige said.

He was already scrolling contacts for Sophie's cell.

"Grant, did you hear what I said?"

"What exactly do you propose we do here, Paige? 'Cause I'm at a loss."

"Call a client."

"Come on."

"It doesn't kill them."

"You don't know what it does. Taking more people into your room isn't a solution."

"I'm not looking for a solution, Grant. I'm just looking to survive the night. I just want this pain to stop."

"Paige—"

"Do I look *well* to you? If I don't get someone upstairs tonight, I won't be alive in the—"

Paige bent over cradling her stomach.

"Paige?"

As Grant moved toward her, she turned and ran.

He limped after her, shouting her name, and as he passed under the archway into the kitchen, he spotted her hunched over the toilet in the bathroom, puking her guts out.

He stepped inside and stood behind her, holding her hair back as she retched into the toilet.

Wasn't the first time.

"It's okay," he said. "You're gonna feel better after this."

She shook her head. She was spitting now, her back heaving up and down as she clambered for a decent breath.

She said, "Hit the light."

Grant did.

The inside of the toilet bowl and everything in the vicinity was dotted with specks of deep burgundy, and over the pungent reek of bile, Grant caught another smell.

Copper.

Blood.

"I'm calling nine-one-one," he said.

"No." Her face was still in the bowl. "They'll try to take me to the hospital. I can't leave the house."

"You just vomited blood."

"Help me get cleaned up."

"Paige—"

"It's either me or someone else. Do you get that yet?"

"We can't go down that road."

"We're there."

Paige sat up and fell back into the wall. She said, "It's that white knight complex that killed your friend. Listen to me for once. Please. You and I are not in control here. I call a client, they come over, I get better. If you bring people to this house, they're going to die. Let me handle this."

Grant looked down at the gore in the toilet. Hard to believe that his sister, small as she was, had that much inside her. Sprawled on the bathroom floor, sheet-white and still dripping with rain and sweat, she looked like a full-on heroin addict.

"All right," he said. "Until I figure out what we're dealing with."

"Give me your phone."

"Why?"

"So I'll know you're one hundred percent with me. So I don't have any more surprise guests showing up at my door."

"You don't trust me?"

"After that stunt you pulled with Don?"

"I'm not giving you my phone."

"Why? Planning on making some calls?"

"It'll make you feel better?"

"Yes."

He tugged his phone out of his pocket, dropped it in Paige's lap.

"Thank you," she said.

She tried to stand, but her arms didn't have the strength to push her onto her feet.

Grant reached down and pulled her up by her hands.

"You know, there's an upside to this approach," she said.

"What's that?"

"Now that you're here, you can see what happens to my clients after I black out."

Paige left the bathroom, and Grant stood at the sink, holding his hands under steaming hot water while he scrubbed every last speck of blood off his hands with a furious focus.

He finally shut off the tap and looked up into the mirror.

He flinched.

Don stared back at him—his face frozen in that moment of grimacing purpose just before he'd opened his throat. His lips didn't move, but

Grant heard his voice as clearly as if his friend had been standing beside him, whispering into his ear.
You don't know anything.
You don't know anything.

Chapter 11

Grant changed into dry clothes—loose-fitting jeans and a T-shirt belonging to one of his sister's clients. He helped Paige clean the wet floors, the bloody upstairs hallway and downstairs bathroom, and generally return the brownstone to the jazz-brimming, candlelit brothel that had greeted him ninety minutes prior.

When the doorbell rang, Grant slipped into an empty closet beside the wet bar, pulling the door closed as Paige moved into the foyer.

She'd skimped down into something so lacy and see-through he could barely bring himself to look at her. But she'd somehow managed to work magic with makeup and foundation, upgrading her appearance from heroin addict to the sexy emaciation of a Paris runway model.

Muffled sounds reached him through the closet door.

Hinges creaked in the foyer.

An exchange of voices, barely discernible, but low and seductive.

Approaching footsteps moved into range, followed by laughter.

Grant heard the clink of ice dropping into empty glasses.

A cork sliding out of a whiskey bottle.

Liquid pouring over cracking ice.

Paige and her client stood at the wet bar, three feet away.

"You look tired, baby," she said, her voice pure saccharine.

"Here's to hoping you can fix that."

Grant's stomach twisted.

"Cheers," the man said.

"Save any lives today?"

"No, actually. Car accident. Couldn't find the hemorrhage in time."

"Sounds like a bad day at the office."

Grant had been fully prepared to despise whoever entered this brownstone with the intention of fucking his sister, but as he eavesdropped from the closet, he couldn't find the rage. He'd stood in this man's shoes countless times. Paid for sex with women who were undoubtedly sisters of other men. Whatever brotherly anger he felt was doomed to be laced with hypocrisy.

"I don't know how you do it, Jude. Life and death every day."

"The good days make it worth it. Also, they pay me a fortune which helps my fragile ego. How you doing, Gloria?"

"Aces."

"Yeah? 'Cause you're looking a little peaked, as my grandmother used to say."

"I'm fine. It's just—"

"Eleven o'clock at night."

"Exactly."

They moved away from the wet bar and Grant heard the squeak of leather as they sat down on the sofa cushions.

In the darkness, he reached down, palmed the doorknob.

Waited for their voices to start up again, then turned it slowly.

When the latch had cleared the housing, he nudged the door open half an inch.

He couldn't see them directly with the door blocking his view, but he could watch their reflection in the big mirror that hung over the fireplace—his sister cuddled into the embrace of a handsome man twenty years her senior. Even sitting, Grant could see that he was tall and endowed with the kind of longish, wavy-gray locks that were made to be windblown behind the wheel of a topless 911.

Grant listened to a conversation that could've unfolded in a confession box—Jude's failing marriage, his suffocating mortgage, his ungrateful children—and all the while Paige gently prodded him along with a sincerity so genuine it made Grant simmer with jealousy. This man was closer to his sister than he was. Eric had been right. She was in a different league. Blue label all the way.

At last, Paige stood and took Jude's hand.

"Come with me," she said.

Jude smiled and rose. "Sure you're up for this tonight? You really look tired," he said.

Paige took a few sultry steps back and waved him on with a finger.

Chapter 12

Grant finally heard the floor upstairs strain under Paige's and Jude's footsteps.

He opened the closet door and headed to the foot of the stairs.

Climbed.

Paige had righted the table in the second-floor hallway and returned the lamp to its original place.

He stopped beside it.

Your friend is dead in a room right around the corner. You should at least put a blanket over him. Something.

Already, he could hear a collection of sounds coming from behind the closed door to Paige's bedroom.

A wooden headboard slapping against the wall.

The low, breathless mumblings of Dr. Jude and his sister.

He involuntarily turned his head.

Despair.

Nausea.

Anguish.

How did you sink this far, baby sis?

He backed away, his eyes locking on the first door he saw, the floor groaning under his weight as he moved toward it.

Get out of sight.

The glass doorknob was freezing to the touch, and while it turned without a problem, the hinges screeched bloody murder. He stared into a linen closet—bare shelves coated with dust and just roomy enough, he hoped, for him to squeeze inside.

Grant stepped in and ducked down, his back flush against the shelves. He reached up and tugged the door shut, but his body blocked it from closing all the way.

The darkness seemed to magnify the labored breathing and muffled friction of the bed frame emanating from Paige's room.

Paige was getting loud and so was Jude.

Grant had just brought his fingers up to plug his ears, when out in the hall, the desk lamp flickered three times.

For a microsecond, it burned as bright as a new star.

Bright enough to blind him and scald the walls with radiance.

It exploded.

The hall went dark.

The acrid stench of ozone and scorched glass filling the air.

Grant strained to listen.

Dead stillness.

His retinas slowly recovering from the overload of light.

He started to push the door open but stopped himself when the bedsprings in Paige's room exhaled a slow groan.

No footsteps followed.

No voices.

The brownstone held its breath, and the longer Grant stood in the closet with the door pulled against his chest, the harder it became for him to move. Fear swept over him, its mass doubling with every pregnant second. He wanted desperately to call out to Paige. His legs began to tremble. A cramp shot through his quads. Sweat beaded on his forehead and slid down into his eyes with a salty sting.

The door to Paige's room swung open.

A figure stood in the doorframe, backlit by candlelight—Jude.

Grant felt the change in his eyes, his chest, his ears—a subtle pulling from the doorway, like a vacuum seal had broken and the room itself was gasping for breath.

He squinted, searching for detail, but Jude was only a profile.

The doctor stepped out into the hall and began to walk, his pace as measured as a metronome, foot-strikes steady even as the glass from the shattered light bulb crunched beneath his feet.

In the darkest part of the corridor, Grant lost his silhouette.

His pulse rate kicked up a notch, eyes working every angle of the crack between the door and its frame for a better perspective.

Four feet from the closet door, Jude reemerged into the scraps of light that filtered up the staircase.

Grant could hear him breathing now and smell his cologne which also bore traces of Paige. Grant struggled to pull the door in with all the force he could rally but it wouldn't close the final inch, leaving a gap that felt as big as the Grand Canyon.

Jude stood in perfect view, the doctor facing the closet door.

Motionless.

Gazing straight at the crack.

For a long time, Jude didn't move.

When he finally stepped forward, his eyes came into the stairway light.

Grant's first thought was that they looked dead, but that wasn't quite right. They exuded a thousand-yard intensity he'd seen countless times during interrogations and interviews. Talking to murderers and victims' next of kin. People who had fucked up or been fucked up and were trying to come to terms with the rest of their life.

Jude took another step toward the closet, so close now that his shadow filled the crack.

The tension coiled in Grant's chest had maxed out its tensile strength.

His system spiked with adrenaline.

Somewhere in the distance, a man began to sing.

Jude stopped, turned his head.

The tinny, five-second refrain of "Ring of Fire" repeated itself from somewhere on the second floor.

Jude's shadow disappeared from the crack, footsteps trailing away while Johnny crooned.

Grant pushed the closet door open.

The hallway was empty, light spilling around the far corner where it had been dark moments before.

Guest bedroom.

Grant bolted down the hall, past the stairwell, forcing himself to slow down as he rounded the corner.

The phone was still ringing, the song much louder.

Grant crept up to the open doorway.

The room stood empty, but there was movement in the bathroom.

Grant took two steps inside, said, "What are you doing?"

The phone went quiet.

Grant saw a shadow stretch across the floor, and then Jude emerged from the bathroom, his white sneakers tracking perfect bloody footprints across the floor. The man stopped and stared at Grant with an expression as lifeless and blank as a mannequin. His hands were darkened with blood, and he held something small and black in his right hand.

Don's cell began to ring again.

Jude raised his arm above his head, and with alarming speed, pitched the phone at the floor.

It shattered against the hardwood in a debris field of glass and plastic and circuitry.

Then Jude started toward him.

Grant instinctively backed away—something in the man's stride putting him on notice.

"I just want to talk to you," Grant said. "I'm Paige's—Gloria's—brother."

Jude didn't stop.

Grant steadied himself, ready to intercept the man if need be, but Jude just stepped to the side and slid past him, their shoulders brushing.

Grant turned and followed him out the door.

"Hey!"

Jude was already halfway down the hall.

Grant doubled his pace.

"I didn't say you could leave."

Jude's gait didn't change, and by the time he reached the top of the stairs, Grant was on his heels.

Jude started down the staircase.

Grant put a hand on his shoulder from behind.

"I'm a cop. That means when I tell you to stop, you listen."

Jude came to an abrupt halt two steps down.

"I want to know what happened in there. In her room."

Jude brought his hand up to his shoulder and wrapped his fingers around Grant's wrist.

Grant tried to jerk his arm away, but the man's grip was a cold vise.

Jude turned and faced him, and the moment he saw Jude's eyes, Grant's words died in his throat.

The man's pupils had been swallowed almost entirely by the roily gray of his irises. Only two infinitesimal pinpricks of black remained, like shrunken keyholes.

Jude folded Grant's wrist back with ease and a lightning bolt of pain exploded up Grant's arm, crumbling him to his knees.

Time protracted, seconds becoming eons of escalating misery as his radiocarpal joint approached its limit. A power surge illuminated the staircase for one burning second, and then everything was enveloped in darkness.

Jude released him.

Grant collapsed onto his side, cradling his hand against his chest as Jude's footsteps continued down the stairs.

"Get back here," he said, but neither his voice nor his heart was in it.

The front door opened and slammed shut, Dr. Jude vanishing into the rainy night.

Chapter 13

"Paige!"

Grant pounded on her door.

"Can you hear me?"

He grabbed the doorknob and tried to turn it, straining with his good wrist until it popped, but nothing happened.

"Paige!"

His voice raced through the second-floor halls that wrapped around the stairwell.

Grant turned and felt his way through the darkness to the hallway table. There was nothing of use on the surface, but a brief exploration along its side revealed a drawer handle.

He yanked it open, blindly rummaging.

Mostly unidentifiable junk.

Couldn't believe his luck when he found a small flashlight.

Please.

He twisted the end and a narrow circle of light shone on the floor beneath him.

Grant returned to the door and dropped to his knees.

Put the side of his head on the hardwood and shined the weak light underneath the crack.

Nothing.

He stood, took several steps back, and accelerated at the door, his shoulder lowered, bracing for impact.

There was as much give as if he'd run straight into a brick wall, a bright shudder of agony exploding in his shoulder and screaming down through his arm to the tips of his fingers.

But a fear that tore his guts out overrode the pain.

Something had happened to Paige and he couldn't get to her.

He sprinted down the hall, around the corner, and shot down the stairs as fast as he could safely travel in the dark.

Need an ax, a sledgehammer, a bowling ball—something with heft.

Failing that, find a toolbox. Physically remove the doorknob.

Grant stopped at the hearth and made a cursory examination of the fireplace toolset. The heaviest thing on the rack was the cast-iron poker, but it wouldn't stand a chance of breaking through Paige's door.

He threw it down and ran into the kitchen.

Pulled open the door to the pantry.

The half-bundle of plastic-wrapped firewood still sat on the floor. He frantically searched the shelves, hoping for a toolbox, a hatchet, something, but the heaviest object he spotted was a thirty-two-ounce can of whole cherry tomatoes.

Think. Think. Think.

As he'd first approached the brownstone after opening the wrought-iron gate, he'd walked up a set of stairs to reach the first level.

Which means—

—there's probably a basement.

Grant shut the pantry door and spun around.

The shock of seeing Paige standing two feet away buckled his knees as if someone had cut his ligaments.

Grant stumbled back against the door.

His sister stared at him—reeking of sex, lingerie badly wrinkled, and looking as bleary and confused as if she'd just woken out of REM sleep.

"Are you all right?" he asked.

She blinked several times without answering, as if the connections between thought and speech were rebooting.

Said finally, "Did you see Jude?"

Grant nodded.
"He left my room?"
"He did a lot more than that."
"Tell me everything."

Chapter 14

The temperature inside the brownstone was diving.

Grant built up the fire with the remaining logs, and with Paige's help, dragged over the leather sofa and the mattress she'd been sleeping on.

He took the flashlight upstairs, stripped the guest bed.

Hauled the pile of blankets and covers downstairs.

It was long past midnight when Grant finally eased down onto the sofa, and as his head hit the pillow, the sheer exhaustion swept through with such intensity he could've mainlined it.

He wrapped two blankets around himself and turned over to face the fire.

The heat felt good, and it came at him in waves.

Paige lay on the mattress several inches below.

"You getting warm?" he asked.

"Not yet. Has it been worse than this?" she asked.

"No, I think we have a winner."

Without the central heat running, it was quiet enough in the powerless house to hear the rain and the occasional hiss of a car going through a puddle on the street, though they were driving by with greater infrequency at this late hour.

Grant pulled his arm out from under the covers and touched Paige's shoulder.

"I can't believe you've been living with this for weeks," he said.

Tears had begun to shine in the corners of her eyes.

"Before," Paige said, "when it was just me, I kept thinking maybe this wasn't real. Maybe I was imagining it. Losing my mind. But now you're here. And don't get me wrong—I'm so glad you are—but it means this is actually happening."

"There's an explanation."

"What?"

"I don't know. But we'll figure it out."

"You're a detective. It's your job to believe there are answers to everything."

"There are answers to everything. Also, I'm very good at my job if that makes you feel any better."

"No offense, but I think haunted houses are a step above your pay grade."

The room undulated in the firelight, Grant so tired his eyes were lingering on the blinks.

"Do you really think this place is haunted?" he asked. "Whatever that even means."

"I've thought about it a lot, and I don't know. But if this *isn't* haunted, I'd hate to see what it takes to qualify."

"How do you sleep knowing what's up there? Or rather, not knowing?"

"I only sleep when my body shuts down and my eyes refuse to stay open. The dreams are awful."

"You have a gun in the house?" he asked.

"Yeah."

"Where is it?"

"My coat pocket. The gray one hanging by the door."

"Loaded?"

"Yes. Why? Planning to shoot a ghost?"

"Never know."

"You know you can't ever go into my bedroom. You know that, right?"

"Yeah."

"Promise me you won't."

"Cross my heart."

For a moment, Grant considered trying to leave again, but just the threat of that all-encompassing pain put a shudder through him.

"I know what you're thinking," Paige said.

"What's that?"

"You're thinking when you wake up in the morning, it'll be different. That there will be light outside and people driving around, and we'll have somehow slept this off."

"I don't know what to think."

She reorganized the covers and tucked them under her feet.

Shut her eyes.

"Don't get your hopes up. You don't wake up from this."

Chapter 15

Two years ago on Thanksgiving night, Grant had questioned a man charged with manslaughter in the death of his wife and children. He'd driven them home drunk from a family dinner and veered head-on into a tow truck. Somehow managed to escape without a scratch.

Grant never forgot how the man had sat in the hard, remorseless light of Interview 3, his head buried in his hands, still fragrant with booze. He wasn't a bad guy. No priors. Had only been moderately drunk. And up until that evening, he'd always been a model family man.

He'd just happened to make a bad choice, catch a tough piece of luck, and ruin his life.

He wouldn't answer questions, wouldn't look at Grant, just kept saying over and over, "I can't believe this is happening. I can't believe this is happening."

Grant had been disturbed by it for a lot reasons, but mostly because he'd driven when he shouldn't have plenty of times.

But for the grace ...

But lying in the firelight as sleep stalked him, he realized he'd never truly understood the sentiment, the horror running through that poor man's mind, until now.

I can't believe this is happening.

Exactly.

It was the feeling, the desperate wish, to go back. To hit undo. To have never walked up the steps to this—haunted?—brownstone. To have never seen Paige's eyes on Facebook. To be anywhere but here—lying on this couch in this cold house under these conditions and Don dead upstairs.

Don is dead.

He hadn't put those words together yet. Hadn't had a chance to.

Now, in the dark with Paige asleep beside him, they came upon him like a freight train out of nowhere, arriving all at once with a truth so big it tripped his breakers.

He felt dizzy, sick.

Don is dead.

It kept repeating in his head—such small words—and yet they were the sound of a lynchpin sliding out. Of Rachel, Don's wife of fifteen years, washing the dinner dishes alone at night in the kitchen before going up to an empty bed.

A new gust of nausea swept over him.

He'd convinced Don to come here.

Grant couldn't handle the stillness any more.

Needed a drink *now*.

He swung his legs over the edge of the sofa and leveraged his weight up, carefully stepping over Paige.

The dying fire provided just enough glow to see the flashlight on the coffee table. He grabbed it and picked his way through the living room, testing each floor plank for noise before committing.

At the wet bar, he reached for the Macallan. Pulled the cork, took a long drink straight from the bottle. It didn't touch his ravenous thirst, but it quenched something so much deeper.

Grant moved through the living room toward the front door.

At the edge of the foyer, he stopped, turned on the flashlight.

Canvassed the room.

Everything in its right place.

Further on in the dining area, the table and ladder-back chairs made a strange geometry of shadows on the wall as the beam passed over them.

Grant stepped into the entryway.

The chill hit him flush on.

What little heat the fire still produced hadn't made it this far.

The staircase loomed just ahead.

Pausing at the bottom, he shined the flashlight up toward the second floor. It didn't quite reach the top, leaving the last few steps in a pool of darkness.

A wash of uneasiness turned his stomach, Grant beginning to second-guess that drink.

He moved closer to the staircase, compelled to scatter the darkness at the top, but just as his foot touched the first step, a thump like a bowling ball dropping on the floor above him shook the house.

He froze, heartbeat thudding in his ears.

Still couldn't see the top of the stairs.

The dining room chandelier swayed in the wake of the noise, tiny glass prisms clinking.

Grant shot a sidelong glance toward Paige in the living room, unwilling to completely tear his eyes or the flashlight away from the staircase.

The firelight was too weak to see her face, but she lay in the same position.

Grant began to climb, each step groaning, and he kept climbing and kept climbing. Knew it wasn't possible—perhaps a symptom of sleep deprivation—but it seemed as if there were twice as many steps as before.

As he approached the top, the floral print of the wallpaper slowly emerged out of the black.

He stepped onto the old carpeting of the second floor and stopped.

The beam of light just a tight circle on the wall straight ahead.

Pure darkness on either side.

He twisted the face cap, hoping for a wider coverage of light, but it only dimmed what little it had to offer.

Grant brandished the flashlight over his shoulder as he moved on and rounded the corner, the hallway illuminating unevenly.

He exhaled.

All quiet.

Paige's bedroom door still closed.

He went on, past the cramped closet where he'd hidden from Jude several hours before, past the table, past Paige's door, and down to the end of the hall where he turned to find the guest bedroom still open, just as he'd left it.

At the doorway, he stopped, resisting an inexplicable urge to enter.

He shined the anemic light into the room.

The stripped bed.

Bits of Don's phone still scattered on the floor.

The bloody footprints.

Horror again at the thought of what had happened in here.

At what lay sprawled across the checkerboard floor of the bathroom.

So why was he walking toward it?

Why was he following those bloody footprints back to their source?

He wanted to stop but didn't.

Couldn't.

The interior of the bathroom swung into view, and he tried to look away, knowing he should just turn off the flashlight, spare himself from seeing this scene again. The images from before had already left an indelible mark. The kind of imprint that would never leave.

But he was already standing in the doorway.

He steadied the light.

The pool of blood where the man had once sat was empty and beginning to congeal imperfectly, like a cracked mirror, black in the feeble illumination of his light.

Don was gone, a sudden confluence of terror and relief flooding through him at the possibility that Don might still be alive.

Grant stepped into the bathroom and crouched down at the edge of the dark puddle.

Passed the light over it.

That's not right, is it?

If Don had somehow gotten up or been moved, the blood would have smeared.

And let's be honest—that is a shit-ton of blood.

Grant stood and traced the floor from the puddle to the doorway with his light. Just the one set of footprints from before—Jude's.

He put his light on the shower curtain.

A prickling sensation dropped down the length of his spine.

Had it been open earlier?

He thought back to his first time in this bathroom, but he couldn't recover the detail. He'd been too focused on his friend.

Grant cocked the flashlight back like a baton as he turned toward the bathtub.

No sound came from behind the curtain.

He stepped forward onto a blood-free section of tile, reached out, caught a fold of fabric between his thumb and forefinger.

He ripped it back.

An empty tub.

The bunched muscles in his shoulders relaxed, but an explosion of footsteps out in the corridor spun him around.

He stepped over the blood, bolted out of the bathroom, and shot through the bedroom toward the open door.

The footsteps pounded down the staircase, shaking the house.

Grant sprinted through the hall above the foyer, screaming his sister's name, screaming for her to wake up.

When he turned the corner, he stopped.

Paige's bedroom door was open.

Blackness inside like he'd never seen.

He felt the mysterious pull.

The rush of air behind him.

He needed his legs to work, to propel him in the opposite direction, but they'd gone lame, and now his knees failed him too.

He was sinking down onto the floor as the room sucked him in, but it wasn't just a physical undertow. He was suddenly aware of something lurking on the outskirts of his consciousness. A concentrated intellect studying the framework of his mind. Searching for a way in. The intensity of its attention like a furnace.

Grant sat up on the living room couch.

His chest billowing.

It took him a moment to recalibrate.

The fire had gone out and the room was freezing.

He reached down and felt for Paige, found her back.

It rose and fell with the unhurried pace of a deep and restful sleep.

Bittersweet reality.

He lay back down and drew the covers up to his neck. The pillow was soaked in sweat and so was he.

Waking up from that nightmare into this one was a small relief, but he'd take it.

He'd take it wherever he could find it.

His pulse rate was falling back toward baseline, and sleep was creeping up on him again like a welcome predator.

No more dreams.

As if he could will such a thing away.

Grant closed his eyes, and they had been shut for less than a second when a sound like a gunshot filled the house.

His eyes opened.

He didn't move because he couldn't.

Frozen with liquid fear.

He stared into the ashen bed of coals beneath the grate, glowing the same subdued color as the brownish-purple dawnlight that was filtering in through the windows.

His heart banged inside his chest with a relentless fury, and he was on the borderline of hyperventilation, his vision sparkling with pulsating specks of black.

That sound.

He knew exactly what it was.

The door to Paige's room had just slammed shut.

Chapter 16

You've reached Grant Moreton. I can't get to the phone right now, but if you'll—

Sophie Benington shelved the handset.

Her sergeant, Joseph Wanger, walked over, looking every bit like the terrifying slob he was—big and broad, his white, button-down oxford hanging out of his waistband, his collar stained with duck sauce the color of radioactivity.

He was tearing through a carton of Chinese food from Grant's second favorite restaurant in the world—the Northgate Panda Express.

When he reached her desk, he rapped his knuckles on the particleboard.

Sophie shook her head.

Wanger sighed heavily and stabbed a plastic fork into the carton. The rippled surface of his shaved head was sweating from the handful of hot mustard packets he'd undoubtedly squeezed onto his meal.

"I've been calling him all morning," Sophie said. "It rings, but he's not picking up."

"You guys are close, right?" His voice pure gravitas and boom. Sophie had seen it break more than a handful suspects, blundering unis who'd muddied the chain of evidence, and even the occasional detective.

"I don't know if I'd say—"

"Come on, Benington. What's going on with your boy?"

"I don't know."

"But you do know Grant's got a taste for scotch. I mean, that don't require any sort of special training to deduce."

"I'm aware, sir."

"He's been fine the last year or two, but he's has not always been the straight and narrow. Any chance he's going through a thirsty spell, and you just don't have the heart to rat him out? It's not a part of your job to protect him, you know."

"I'm not protecting him."

Wanger shoveled a pile of lo mein noodles into his mouth, his massive black mustache glistening with MSG.

"Look, I've known Grant for two years," Sophie said. "He's shown up for work hung-over a few times."

"A few?"

"A few times a week. Rolled in still drunk once or twice. But he's never *not* shown up."

"Boy could be going through some shit not on your radar."

"I don't think so."

"So you guys *are* all cuddly then?"

She imagined lifting the paperweight off her desk—a viceroy butterfly enclosed in a clear globe—and smashing it into Wanger's ball sack.

"No, but I do sit across from the man every day. I wouldn't be a good detective if I couldn't tell if something was bothering my own partner, would I?"

"So does this mean you're worried?"

"Yes."

"And you've tried him at home?"

"His cell is the only way to reach him. I also texted him and sent him an e-mail. No response. I was thinking of driving over to his apartment in Fremont."

Wanger was already nodding as he chewed.

"Do it," he said. "Right now."

Sophie stood at Grant's door on the third floor of his townhome walkup. The building was nice, but Grant had about as much design sense as a monk.

She pounded on his door again.

"Grant! *You in there?*"

No answer.

Turning away, she pushed the thought out of her mind that he was lying dead in there. She had circled the surrounding blocks several times, but couldn't find his black Crown Vic. At least that was something.

Halfway down the last flight of stairs, her phone rang—Detective Dobbs calling. She answered as she moved past the mailboxes and toward the front door.

"What's up, Art?"

"I just got a strange call. A groundskeeper spotted a man in the Japanese garden at the Washington Park Arboretum."

"So what?"

"Silver responded. Turns out it's Benjamin Seymour, your missing lawyer."

"So Seymour's okay?"

"Not exactly."

"What does that mean?"

"Just go see for yourself."

Sophie pushed open the front door and headed down the concrete steps toward her silver TrailBlazer which she'd double-parked in front of the building.

"I'm on my way," she said.

"Where are you?"

"Fremont. Have Bobby keep eyes on him."

"Any word on Grant?"

"I'm just leaving his apartment. He isn't here."

"Your boy'll turn up. Probably just tripped over a big night."

"Hey, Art?"

"Yeah?"

Her car alarm chirped.

"He's not my boy."

"If you say so."

Chapter 17

Grant could see that he was standing on two feet, but it didn't feel that way. He'd had his share of I-feel-like-death hangovers in recent years, but nothing approaching this. His head felt like the Liberty Bell—deeply cracked—and a pool of something in his stomach was threatening to surface.

He stepped over his still-sleeping sister onto the frigid hardwood floor and made a mad dash to the bathroom off the kitchen.

Knees hit tile, and he just managed to throw open the toilet seat before spewing his guts into the bowl.

He flushed.

Hauled himself up.

Cranked open the faucet and rinsed his mouth and spit.

He'd had a few drinks the night before, but he didn't deserve this.

Grant turned the water off and straightened. His back cracked. He dug the crust from the corners of his lids with a knuckle and checked his reflection in the mirror—eyes sunken and red-veined, hair like something out of an eighties music video.

He ran a hand over the scratch of fresh beard.

Something about his face seemed off. After a night of too much booze and restless sleep, he could faithfully count on swollen cheeks and puffy eyes. But this morning, nothing about him looked bloated. His face was as thin as he'd seen it in years. Verging into gaunt.

He walked through the kitchen and up the hallway into the foyer.

Unlocked the front door, stepped out onto the porch.

His ears popped from that persistent pressure gradient.

The rain had stopped and the air smelled of wet pavement. The sky hadn't cleared, but the clouds overhead were thin enough for the incoming sunlight to burn his eyes. It was a suddenly warm Friday for December and people would be pouring out of their homes and into the green spaces with the kind of shared satisfaction that only rainy cities relish on days like this.

A woman ran by pushing a jogger-stroller.

The streets hummed with traffic.

The hedges dripped.

Wind pushed the scent of a distant coffee shop his way.

He glanced at his watch—later than he thought. They'd slept past noon.

His fingernails looked dirty, but he knew it wasn't that.

Don's blood.

The despair and heartache nearly brought him to his knees.

The view off the front porch was panoramic—Lake Union spread out before him, a fleet of sailboats and kayaks speckling its grey surface with color. The Cascades were still socked in. Farther up on the north bank, the hulking ruins of Gas Works Park loomed over squares of bright, rain-fresh grass like the skyline of a steampunk novel. Grant couldn't see the people, but he imagined them on picnic blankets, children scrambling up the hill, dragging kites in the breeze behind them.

He drew in a deep breath.

Took a step down.

Then another.

As if this day was just something he could walk out into.

What had been a dull, painless throbbing behind his eyes ratcheted up a few degrees until it felt like someone was rolling his optic nerve between two meaty fingers.

He descended two more steps.

The meaty fingers became a poking needle.

His stomach contracted into a ball of molten iron, and the agony doubled him over, Grant clutching his gut as he tried to backpedal up the steps.

By the time he reached the landing, clawing desperately for the door, the pain had begun to moderate.

Grant stumbled back into the gloom of Paige's brownstone.

His sister was sitting up on the mattress in the living room, her knees drawn into her chest.

"How far did you get?" she asked.

"Two steps from the bottom."

Grant made his way over to the couch and collapsed onto it.

"Did you throw up yet?" she asked. "That's how I start the morning these days."

"First thing."

"It's not a hangover."

"I know."

"It only gets worse."

"Is this you trying to help?"

"Sorry."

"It's warmer outside than it is in here," Grant said.

"I think it's your body temperature, not just the house. Chills?"

Grant hadn't noticed chills specifically amid the grocery list of other symptoms, but he did feel feverish.

"Yeah. I'm gonna build a fire."

"We're out of firewood."

"We aren't out of furniture." He sat up, wrapped the covers around his shoulders. "What's going on in this house, Paige?"

"I don't know."

"No idea."

"None."

"Nothing weird has happened to you lately that you're forgetting to tell me?"

"Like what?"

"Oh, I don't know. You haven't desecrated any sacred Indian burial grounds lately, have you?"

"Not lately."

"No deals with some guy in a red lounge suit holding a garden tool?"

She just smiled.

"So what then?" Grant asked.

"I don't know. This isn't a Halloween special."

"You've been living with this thing for a month."

"Well aware."

"So what do *you* think it is?"

She shook her head.

"No matter what you say, I won't judge you."

"You remember going to church with Mom and Dad?"

"Barely."

"Remember how it was only ever about Satan and demons?"

"That's *all* I remember about it."

"Me too, and it scared me atheist. When we stopped going after Mom died, I still couldn't get that stuff out of my head."

"I remember your nightmares."

"Right," Paige said. "They were horrible. I used to dream that this demon I could never see was crawling down the hall toward our bedroom. I knew it was coming, but I couldn't move. My legs had stopped working. Its shadow—Jesus, it still creeps me out big time—would stop in the doorway behind me. I could feel it standing there, and every time I tried to sit up and turn around to see it, I'd wake up."

"That's pretty standard nightmare material."

"But that's what these last four weeks have felt like. The same kind of fear—of being alone in a house, but knowing you aren't really alone."

"And not being able to do anything about it, including leaving."

"Exactly. It's this helpless, claustrophobic feeling."

"So you think it's something demonic?"

"I don't know. All I'm saying is that it feels like the kind of thing I used to be afraid of."

"Have you called anyone?"

"Who would I call?"

"A professional."

"You mean like an exorcist?"

"I know, I can't believe I'm suggesting it."

Paige cocked her head. "You think we should?"

Grant didn't want to say it. Every ounce of training, years of collecting facts and scrutinizing them screamed that there was a corporeal explanation here that could be booked down at the station. He based his life, his choices, on empirical evidence. Aristotle and all that shit.

"It doesn't matter whether we believe in it or not," he said. "There's something happening in this house and it doesn't look like we're equipped to deal with it. I say we bring someone in. You got a phone book?"

"In the kitchen."

"I could use some coffee now that I mention it."

"We still don't have power."

"You have a French press?"

"Nope."

"No worries. Long as you've got the beans, I can save the day."

Chapter 18

Grant opened the gas on one of the back burners and struck a match. It ignited with a whoomf and settled down into a neat blue circle of quietly-hissing flame. He set a copper-bottomed pot filled with tap water onto the burner.

"Whole bean all you got?" he said, peering into the stainless steel canister where Paige kept her stash.

"Sorry."

He thought for a moment.

"You have anything made of silk?"

A few minutes later, Grant was pouring a handful of beans into one of Paige's socks and beating them into grounds with a meat pulverizer.

On the other side of the kitchen, his sister was fishing through a drawer jammed to bursting with junk that either didn't have a home or had fallen out of use—a refuge of forgotten toys.

Paige fished out the fat Seattle phone book, let it thud against the counter.

"Haven't seen one of these in awhile," she said.

It was waterlogged and dogeared. Grant imagined it sitting on the front steps like a lost kitten for days in the rain before Paige had finally surrendered and brought it inside.

She fanned it open.

"E for exorcist?" she asked.

"I guess."

Grant looked over her shoulder as she thumbed back to the yellow pages.

"It's not in the Es."

"Don't priests handle these things? Maybe we can talk to whoever's in charge of whatever-the-hell parish we're in."

"It's so easy in the movies," she said, prying the pages apart. "They make it sound like there's this whole industry. Okay, here we go. St. James Cathedral. It's that big church on First Hill. Bunch of phone numbers."

Grant scrolled the list with his finger.

"Not seeing anything related to exorcism. What about demonologist?" he said.

"Is that a real thing?"

"I think so."

Paige flipped through the Ds.

"Nope. No wonder people don't use phone books anymore."

"You think it'd be possible for me to get my phone back?"

"Why?"

"So I can call the church. Uh-oh."

"What?"

"Seriously. Go get my phone."

"What's wrong?"

"Did you turn it off when I handed it over last night?"

"I don't remember."

"You understand that when we run out of battery power, we're pretty much cut off from the outside world in here."

Paige rushed into the living room. Grant heard a drawer squeak open, papers shuffling. She came back holding his phone and hers.

"You've got a little less than a quarter of a charge," she said. "And fourteen missed calls from someone named Sophie." Her right eyebrow went up. "Lady friend?"

He grabbed his phone.

"She's my partner."

"Well, it looks like she cares."

"Everyone at the station is probably wondering where I am. How much battery life do you have?"

"Half."

"Let me have yours."

"Why?"

He slid open the back of his phone, popped out the battery, set it on the granite countertop.

"Because people can track me to your house if this phone is running." Paige handed over her phone. "Can you get me that number?" he asked.

She flipped back to the listing for St. James Cathedral and called it out.

An elderly-sounding woman answered on the second ring, "St. James."

Grant put the phone on speaker and set it face-up on the kitchen island.

"Hi, who am I speaking with please?"

"This is Gertrude. What can I do for you?"

"I was trying to reach the parish priest."

"Just a moment."

The hold Muzak was a Gregorian chant.

After thirty seconds, a soft-spoken man answered, "Jim Ward."

"Hi Jim, my name's Grant."

"How can I help you, Grant?"

"My sister and I are dealing with an issue in her house."

As Grant listened to the long pause on the other end of the line, it occurred to him that he didn't have the first idea of how to say this.

The priest finally nudged him on. "Could you elaborate?"

"I think we have some kind of—I don't know—entity."

"Entity?"

"Yes." He hoped the priest would take the ball and run with it, spare Grant the humiliation of having to provide a blow-by-blow for something that was sounding more ridiculous every second.

"I'm afraid I don't quite understand what you mean."

"There's something upstairs that is … I don't really know how to put this … not of this world."

An even longer pause.

Grant stared at Paige across the kitchen island.

"I know this sounds weird," Grant said. "I promise you it's not a joke. I couldn't be more serious or more in need of help."

"Are you a member of St. James?" the priest asked.

"No, sir."

"Is your sister?"

"No."

"What exactly is it that you would like for me to do?"

"To be honest, I don't have the first clue about where to begin with something like this. I was hoping you would."

"Do you believe this is demonic activity you're dealing with?"

"I don't know. I think it might be."

"We're really not equipped for this in any of our Seattle parishes, but there is a priest trained in the rite of exorcism in Portland."

"Could you put us in touch?"

"There's a protocol for these types of matters. It's just you and your sister?"

"Yes."

"And do you suspect possession?"

"I'm sorry?"

"Do you believe this entity has control over you or your sister?"

Grant met eyes with Paige.

"I don't know."

"I would be happy to meet with both of you. I'm booked up today, but you could come by my office first thing Monday."

"What's this priest's name? The one in Portland?"

"The better course of action would be to have you meet with me first. Then I could make a referral."

Grant said, "That won't work for us. I want you to take down our address. It's Twenty-two Crocket Street in upper Queen Anne—the freestanding brownstone on the corner. Please communicate to this priest in Portland that we need to see him."

"If this is a true emergency, I could come by myself after I leave the office tonight."

"Are you equipped to handle something like this, Father?"

A brief pause and then: "Well, it's not exactly a science, but I'm not the best suited for this type of thing, no."

"Then don't come here alone. Give the address to the other priest or don't do anything."

"I'll see what can be done."

"Thank you."

Grant gave him his phone number and hung up.

The water was boiling on the stove.

He walked over and lifted the pot off the gas.

"That guy isn't sending anybody," Paige said.

"You're probably right."

Grant emptied the silk sock filled with fresh coffee grounds into the hot water. He stirred them in with a wooden spoon and topped the pot with its lid.

"You're looking pale," Paige said.

Grant nodded. He felt dizzy too, and his headache was becoming impossible to ignore.

"It was a long night. I just need some coffee," he said.

"Coffee won't fix this. Should I run through the list of symptoms? I know them pretty well."

"I'll be fine."

"You'd have to be a pretty bad detective to actually believe that."

She was right, but he wasn't ready to give up on the hope that his headache and sour stomach were just the parting gifts from a terrible evening followed by an even worse night's sleep.

"This is just the beginning. You have no idea how bad it's about to get."

Paige walked over to the pot and lifted the lid. Pungent curls of steam made a brief appearance before dissipating. She picked up the wooden spoon and gave the darkening liquid a few stirs.

"I've been where you're at," she said. "Wanting to hold off. Thinking I could control my own deterioration."

"I'm not sending another person up there, Paige. If that's what you're getting at."

"But when it was me hurting, that was—"

"Different, yes." Grant leaned against the counter.

"Because it's okay as long as *I'm* the one needing help?" she asked.

"Because my sister was dying."

She let the spoon clatter to the counter and turned to face him.

"It wants someone else, Grant. Do you think I can't feel it too? Do you think it won't bring me to my knees all over again if we hold off? You saw how I looked last night. I'll be just as bad off, if not worse, in another twelve hours."

"We can't keep sending men up there. Who knows where they're going, what they're doing, when they leave your brownstone."

"I don't like it either. You may not understand, but these men are more than just clients to me."

"I get that." *More than you know.*

"Look, we can put this off now, but there will come a time—I promise you—when you beg me to bring someone over. I don't want either of us to get to that point."

Grant circled the island and took a seat on one of the stools. He crossed his arms on the cool tile and let his head fall onto them. Felt like his brain had been submerged in a bucket of ice water. Each thought arrived cut into slices, and as Grant struggled to assemble them, the only thing that surfaced out of his fog was that she was right—he couldn't hold out forever.

Paige came over to him.

"You know we don't have a choice," she said softly. "But there's a good reason to do it soon."

"What's that?" he said without lifting his head.

The room had become thick with the rich aroma of coffee. On any other day, that smell alone would have been sufficient to give Grant a pleasant dopamine pregame in anticipation of the real thing. Now it struck him as flat and unappealing.

"I just thought of it this morning," she said. "Don't know why it didn't occur to me before." She ran her fingers through his hair. "We have a chance to learn something about that thing that's living in my room."

For a brief second, curiosity broke through the mounting pain. Grant heaved his head off the cool comfort of the tile.

"How?"

"It's kept me a prisoner for two weeks, and I still don't know anything about it."

"Because you're always unconscious when it shows up."

"And when it's all over, my client's gone and I don't have a clue about what happened. Tonight will be different. We're going to make a video of the whole thing."

"With what?"

"My phone. I'll leave it on the dresser. There's no reason my client will think to look for it. His mind will be on other things."

Grant considered this. Concrete visual evidence was exactly what they needed, and not just for themselves, but for any help that eventually showed up. At the very least, it was more of a plan than anything they'd had up until now. But the idea of watching his sister with another man was beyond what he could handle. Listening to them last night had been hard enough.

"That's good," he said finally. "We need intel on what we're dealing with."

Grant struggled onto his feet, went to the stove.

"Coffee?" he said.

"Please."

He pulled two mugs down from their hooks underneath the cabinets and slid a coffee filter over the top of each one. Lifting the pot, he poured over the paper, careful to avoid a scalding splash as the grounds collected and the holy, black liquid passed through the paper.

"Smells like coffee," Paige said.

He carried the warm mugs over to the island.

"This is how the cowboys rolled," he said, placing one of the cups in front of his sister.

"We even have a whorehouse."

"Can't stop yourself, can you?" he asked.

"From what?"

"Pressing every last button you see."

"You do have a lot of them."

They drank, not minding the bitter grinds that had escaped the filter.

"Not bad," Paige said.

"It'll do in a pinch."

"We're in one."

For just a moment, the simple act of holding the steaming mug made things feel slightly better. A small, familiar thing in the midst of an alien chaos. Their world may have been upended, but he could still make a cup of coffee.

He said, "It might not work, you know. Video might show us nothing."

"Pessimistic much?"

"I'm not saying we don't do it. We just can't hang our hat on one thing. We need to do more."

"Like what?"

"There was this woman we brought in on a murder case several years ago."

"You mean like a psychic?"

"No, she got really upset if you called her that. She billed herself as a trance medium, whatever the hell that means. And yes, she's even weirder than it sounds."

"Did she help?"

"I don't know. *She* seemed to think so, although the case was never solved. I might call her."

"Why?"

"Because we're desperate." He slugged back a big swallow of coffee. "You know, if this were a haunted house movie—"

"It's not."

"But if it were, our job would be to find out what happened in this house."

"What do you mean?"

"You know how some tragic event always precipitates a haunting? Like a murder?"

"I can't quite believe we're having this conversation. Those are film tropes, Grant. What's happening to us is real."

"Then what do you want to do?"

She stared at him, frustrated. Shook her head finally, said, "I don't know."

"Then let's at least *do* something. Maybe it works. Maybe it doesn't. At least we'll be trying. Isn't that the whole point of your video?"

"Fine."

"So what do you know about this house?"

"Nothing. I moved in two months ago."

"Well, we need to find out everything we can."

"You mean like if the prior resident was an insane caretaker who murdered his entire family?"

"Yes, that kind of thing. We're sort of stranded here, but I have a friend I can call."

"Who?"

"He's a private investigator."

"Grant, I know we need a little outside help, but this isn't going to come back to bite me in the ass, is it?"

"What do you mean?"

"I can't have people digging into my private life."

"Paige, this guy's a friend."

"Still."

"And more importantly, the last guy in the world to cast a stone."

"Okay. I trust you."

"Then let's make some calls."

Grant picked up the battery to his phone, reassembled everything, and powered it up.

"I thought they could track you with that."

"I just need to get those numbers for the PI and the freakshow."

As he scrolled through contacts, the phone began to vibrate in his hand. "Damn," he said.

"Who is it?"

He set the phone on the tile, Sophie's name burning across the screen. Paige said, "You got the numbers. Turn it off."

He shook his head.

"I'm thinking that's not the right play. Sophie isn't going to stop. It's not in her programming."

"So what are you going to do?"

He picked up the phone.

"I'm going to talk to her."

Chapter 19

Sophie walked through the entrance gate and up the paved walkway into the garden. She'd made it a habit last summer of coming here on pretty Sundays, but despite the patches of blue sky above, in its present state, the garden felt a far cry from the lushness of July. Winter had muted its color to shades of grey and evergreen, and something inside of her hated seeing it this way—like staring down at her mother in the casket—there but not.

A groundskeeper stood under a leafless Japanese maple, a bulging trash bag at his feet. Sophie opened her wallet as she approached, but the man didn't bother to examine her credentials.

"Detective Sophie Benington," she said. "I understand you discovered Mr. Seymour this morning?"

The groundskeeper leaned against the handle of his rake, sweat stains reaching from his armpits down the sides of his uniform.

A tall, skinny kid with ropey dreads and gentle eyes.

"He was sitting on the bench by the pond when I got here."

"And you've never seen him in the garden before?"

"No, we keep this part of the arboretum closed in the winter. We occasionally have to chase out a few homeless and freegans, but mostly this place stays dead."

Sophie moved on past the groundskeeper toward Officer Silver. He stood fifty yards up the path in his dark blue uniform, and as the sound of Sophie's Frye boots clicking against the pavement pulled within range, he turned and watched her approach.

The man was tall but he looked about eighteen years old, with the creamy complexion and boring good looks of a high school jock.

"Hey, new guy," she said.

Silver smirked. He'd actually been with SPD longer than Sophie, but as bad nicknames are wont to do, his had stuck.

"Seymour's right out there?" she asked.

"Yeah."

Just beyond where they stood, the trees opened up. There was the pond—brown and still—with a little bridge going across the middle. Sophie could just see the back of a head poking up from behind a cluster of bushes.

"What are you gonna do?" Silver asked.

"I'm not sure yet."

"Something's off with this guy. Want me to come with?"

"Not yet."

"He could be dangerous, Sophie."

"Jeez, he really creeped you out, huh?"

"Yeah, actually."

"Hang back, but stay close."

Sophie followed the meandering path along the north bank of the pond. The garden was steeped in solitude, and except for the distant murmur of traffic, Sophie's footfalls were the only noise that violated the serenity of the place.

She couldn't shake the feeling that it was wrong to be here with the trees skeletal and devoid of color. Even worse to be here on the job.

She stopped.

Ten yards ahead, past a grove of rhododendron, she spotted a pair of benches.

One was empty.

Benjamin Seymour sat motionless on the other.

He could have been a garden feature, his stillness matched by the Zen landscape. After three days of staring at photographs of him taken in better times, it was strange to see him sitting there in the actual like a statue.

She reached into her jacket and unsnapped her holster, let her palm rest on the stock of her G22. After coming on board with CID, she'd had belt loops sewn into all of her pants since the hip rig dragged them down. Much preferred the way this belted holster rode on her hips.

She hailed the man from a few paces away—better to make her presence known than risk startling him.

"Mr. Seymour?"

He didn't move.

"I'm Detective Benington with the SPD. Everything okay?"

Seymour casually stretched his arm across the back of the bench but made no response.

"I'm coming over, Mr. Seymour."

Sophie entered the rhododendron grove.

From a distance, Seymour could have been any park patron stopped for a contemplative moment by the pond. In proximity, the red flags began to wave. His custom-made suit was soaked through, and his hair had long since lost its gelled structure. It would have taken hours for the light Seattle rain to do this level of damage.

"Can you hear me, Mr. Seymour?"

He looked over at her and blinked, a galactic distance in his eyes.

"Where have you been for the past three days?" she asked.

"Here."

"You've been sitting on this bench for over seventy-two hours?"

"The gardens are beautiful in winter."

"They're also closed. You're trespassing."

"I didn't realize. I apologize. I'll leave."

He started to rise.

"Wait a moment. Just stay where you are. Are you injured?"

He sat down, looked back at the pond. "No."

"Are you on any drugs right now?"

"No."

"Are you carrying any weapons I should know about?"

He shook his head.

"People have been looking for you. They're worried."

"That's very kind."

Sophie ventured a step closer.

The man was shivering imperceptibly.

"What are you doing out here, Mr. Seymour?"

"Thinking. It's a good place for it."

"What are you thinking about?"

He didn't answer.

The wind kicked up.

A scrap of paper in Seymour's right hand twitched in the breeze. In his other hand, he held a pen.

"What's that paper, Mr. Seymour?"

No response.

Sophie edged closer.

"Could I take a look?"

When he didn't respond, she slowly reached down and eased the paper out of his grasp. Sophie took several steps away from the bench and glanced back toward the main path. Silver had moved closer, now standing only twenty yards away, watching intently.

She looked down at the crumpled paper in her hand—a receipt for a twenty-five-dollar pour of Highland Park at a downtown bar called The Whisky.

The time stamp was 5:11 p.m., three days ago.

She looked up at him again.

Seymour stared past her into oblivion.

Sophie flipped the receipt over.

In rain-smeared ink, the visage of an old man stared back at her. What the portrait lacked in artistic flair was counterbalanced by a staggering detail that reminded her of a facial composite. It was an expertly-executed sketch, but as impersonal as a mugshot.

"Did you draw this, Mr. Seymour?"

"Yes."

"Who is it?"

"I don't know."

"Did you see this man somewhere?"

"Yes."

"Where?"

"In my head."

"Did this man hurt you?"

"No, I've never met him."

Sophie slid the receipt into an inner pocket of her jacket.

"What do you remember about being at The Whisky three nights ago?" she asked.

Seymour started to rise.

She took a step back and touched her gun.

Silver shouted, "Everything okay?"

"We're fine," she yelled, her eyes never leaving Seymour.

Seymour buttoned his jacket.

"I'm sorry for any trouble I've caused."

"What happened to you?"

"The gardens are beautiful this time of year, aren't they?" he said with an empty smile that was completely disconnected from his eyes.

He started up a slope of browned grass.

Sophie followed.

"Mr. Seymour, please. You need to go to a hospital."

The man reached the path and continued walking toward the entrance gate.

"What happened?" Silver asked.

"I have no idea. Walk with me."

"You're letting him go?"

"What exactly would you propose we bring him in on?"

"Trespassing."

"Please."

"At least you'll get a chance to talk to him."

"He isn't giving anything up. I got stonewalled."

"What do you think happened to him?"

"Nervous breakdown? Drugs? Some kind of trauma?"

"So we're just going to watch him walk away?"

"Of course not." Seymour passed through the entrance gate to the Japanese garden as Sophie dug her phone out of her purse. "I'm going to follow him."

Chapter 20

"Don't," Paige said.

Grant touched his finger to the screen.

"We have to buy ourselves some time."

Paige clenched her jaw.

"Fine. Put her on speaker."

Grant swiped the screen, activated the speaker, and set the phone back on the island.

"Sophie," he said.

"Jesus Christ, Grant. Wanger's practically interviewing for your replacement. Where are you?"

"On my way home from the hospital."

The words had left his mouth before he'd even given it a thought—a reflexive lie.

"Oh my God, what happened?"

The concern in her voice shot a hollowpoint of guilt through his chest. He felt it mushroom center mass. He'd never lied to Sophie before. Never had a reason to. Six months into their partnership, she'd had Grant down so cold she could have reconstructed him from junk parts. Now, after sharing a desk for two years, he could say as much. They operated on the same frequency, and that was the problem. Her bullshit meter was a finely calibrated tool. If his performance wasn't Oscar material, she'd know it.

He glanced at Paige, her eyes gone wide, head slowly shaking like *what-are-you-going-to-say-now?*

"Let's just say that the Spicy Italian is no longer my favorite sandwich."

Something like a snort crackled over the speaker.

"Was that a laugh?" Grant said.

"No, I promise," Sophie laughed.

"You are so cruel."

"I just can't believe you got food poisoning from Subway. That's just … wow. Do you need anything?"

"Rest."

"You should've called me."

"Kind of hard when they're pumping your stomach."

"Oh, sweetie, I'm sorry."

Paige raised an eyebrow.

Grant rolled his eyes.

"Can I bring you something?" Sophie asked. "Your favorite sub? I'm sorry, that was too soon."

"No, I'm drained. Just going home to crash. Might take the next few days off. "

"That's not a bad idea. You sound awful."

"Would you tell Wanger for me?"

"Sure, but you're going to hate your timing."

Grant looked up at Paige.

"What's going on?"

"We found Benjamin Seymour."

Porcelain and coffee exploded on the floor beside Grant's feet.

Paige's eyes filled with terror, hands still clutching the shape of the mug that lay in pieces on the hardwood.

Grant mouthed to his sister, *What?*

She shook her head and pointed at the phone.

"What was that?" Sophie asked.

"Sorry. Hit a pothole."

The pool of coffee was expanding toward Grant's socks.

Paige collected herself, grabbed the dishcloth from the oven handle, and began blotting the liquid.

"Alive?" Grant asked.

"Yes."

"Where'd you find him?"

"At the arboretum. I'm here now. He'd apparently been sitting on a bench for days before a groundskeeper found him and called it in. I tried talking to him but the guy's a space cadet. Virtually catatonic. Could barely respond. Just sat there staring at the water."

"So he was on something?"

"I don't think so. It was more like he was sleepwalking."

"So you're bringing him in?"

Thinking, *He'll lead them straight to me and Paige.*

"No. I'm going to follow him. Something's up. He was holding a drawing he'd done on a receipt. A hyper-realistic portrait of an old man's face. I've got it with me. This thing is amazing, Grant. Our boy's an artist."

"Seymour drew it?"

"That's what he said."

"Who's the old man?"

"He didn't know. Said he'd never met him."

"That sounds like eight kinds of strange."

Paige had finished soaking up the coffee, now picking up fragments of the mug.

"Well, don't figure it all out before I get back," Grant said.

"I don't think there's any danger of that. This is a weird one. Sure I can't bring you something?"

"No, but you're my first call if I change my mind."

"All right, partner. Feel better. I'll keep you looped in."

Grant clicked off.

His heart pounding.

Paige had opened the cabinet under the sink and was dumping the broken cup into a trashcan. She closed the door and stood, looked back at Grant, her face as white as the porcelain shards.

"You all right?" he asked.

"Benjamin Seymour is one of mine. He came here three nights ago."

"And it went down just like with the doctor last night?"

She nodded.

"Was a man named Barry Talbert also a client of yours?"

"Yeah, why?"

"He's missing too. I'm sure you're aware, but these are prominent, wealthy men in the business and legal community."

"That's who I service."

"SPD is looking extra hard for them. The search for these men is what led me to your Facebook page in the first place. It's going to be a matter of time before the entire investigative division—" Grant tapped the surface of the island "—knocks on the door."

"So what do we do if it happens? If your buddies show up?"

"We can't let that happen, okay? Think about what it would look like to a cop walking in here, finding Don upstairs. Now think about how it would sound if you and I tried to explain any of this. I wouldn't buy it for a second."

"You sound scared."

"I am scared. Of whatever's upstairs, and what could happen if the cavalry shows up. We're in a bad spot here."

Grant lifted his phone and stared at the screen.

The battery meter had dwindled into the yellow.

"So what do we do?" Paige asked.

"A Hail Mary."

He scrolled his contacts down to *stu*.

Dialed.

A gruff-voiced man answered immediately, "G, what's happening?"

"Stu, need a big favor."

"Did I miss when you called for a little one?"

Grant hesitated, fighting through the pounding headache to pin down the best way to ask.

"I need everything you can dig up on an address."

"That doesn't sound too bad."

"I need it in four hours."

"Okay, that's not even a rush job, Grant. That's like—"

"I don't care what it—"

"You know my rush jobs are double."

"Aware."

"We're talking triple here. At least. I'm going to have to drop some high priority cases."

"I don't care what it costs."

Through the speaker, Grant heard paper ripping, the murmur of a crowd, music, a distant, mechanical grinding that could only be espresso beans on their way to a small, white cup. An image materialized—Stu at his "office." A coffeehouse in Capital Hill.

Stu said, "What's the address?"

"Twenty-two Crockett Street."

"Queen Anne?"

"Correct."

"Give me your wish list."

"Every owner going back twenty years. Every tenant going back twenty years. Background checks all around. And finally, assuming this property was sold in the last twenty years, I want a copy of the seller's disclosure form."

"That last one may be impossible, Grant."

"Just try."

"Those aren't public records. I can't just go down to the clerk and recorder's office and pull that. Now I have contacts at two of the biggest title companies in town. Assuming there was a sale, and that one of those companies issued title insurance, it's conceivable I could get my hands on the disclosure statement. Just don't count on it. But look, regardless, there's no way I'll have all this information to you in four hours. There's only three hours left in this work week. It's an impossib—"

"Just get me what you can get me." Grant pulled the phone back, glanced at the time: 1:55 p.m. "I need it by six tonight. I'll be out of pocket until then. Call me at six exactly with whatever you've got."

"Grant—"

"I understand. No warranty on you delivering all of this. But please just do what you can. I'm in a jam here."

Stu sighed heavily into the receiver.

"I'll see what I can do."

"Six p.m. exactly."

Grant axed the call.

Battery meter in the red.

He powered off his phone and looked at Paige. Already, she was tapping at her phone.

She brought it to her ear and faced the window over the double sink, her back to Grant.

It was the voice that took him aback, his sister transforming on a dime into this other person, her voice disintegrating.

From woman to girl.

Pitch rising.

Words drawing out.

It injured his soul.

"Hey sweetie, this a good time? … Nothing much. Just thinking about you, wondering how your week's been. Almost over, right? … Look, I've got some time after six tonight if you wanted to swing by."

Chapter 21

Sophie crossed Lake Washington and Mercer Island, blasting east on 90 toward the Cascades as she followed the white Lexus that Seymour was piloting twenty car lengths ahead.

It hummed along at a rock-solid sixty miles-per-hour.

Douglas-firs streamed past.

The cloud deck dropped.

Specks of mist starring the windshield.

She was sixty percent focused on the Lexus two hundred feet ahead, forty percent elsewhere.

More specifically: *Grant.*

My partner.

Are you lying to me? Just the thought of it hurt her more than she was comfortable admitting. Like it was a betrayal on some level beyond partner. Beyond friend.

A blinking right turn signal on Seymour's Lexus snapped her back into the moment. He was already on the off-ramp.

Sophie pressed the accelerator into the floorboard and followed him off the exit.

Two minutes later, she was rattling over train tracks into downtown North Bend, a slice of Americana so well-preserved she felt her very presence threatened its legitimacy. She rarely left the city. So easy to forget that places like this existed just thirty minutes outside of Seattle proper.

The Lexus pulled into the near-desolate parking lot of Swartwood's Diner.

Sophie turned into the alley that cut behind the building and pulled her TrailBlazer to a stop beside a mural on the white concrete of the back wall.

Through the driver's side window, she watched Seymour climb out of his Lexus and walk toward the entrance to the diner.

She couldn't explain it exactly, but she felt jittery, like she'd just downed a quad-shot espresso concoction. Everything about Seymour felt wrong. He was uncharted territory, and it made her feel like a rookie again—those first days on the street and coming to grips with the utter inadequacy of textbook knowledge.

Sophie reached into her jacket and pulled her G22, checked the load.

More nervous tic than necessity.

She put the SUV back into gear.

Drove down the alley and around the block.

She parked at a better location in front of the entrance.

Seymour had taken a booth by the window. His back was to her.

Good visibility, lucky break.

She killed the engine, reclined the seat.

It got boring in a hurry.

A waitress appeared at Seymour's table.

Left.

Returned with coffee.

Seymour never glanced out the window beside his booth. Never brought the steaming cup to his lips. He had cleaned himself up since their encounter at the park—presumably in his car considering she hadn't let him out of her sight. But other than an argyle sweater, fresh pair of jeans, and immaculate hair, he was the same old catatonic Seymour.

The rain fell so lightly it took almost forty-five minutes to blur her view through the windshield.

When she could no longer see through it, she opened the car door and climbed out.

The smell of fir trees was overpowering.

A mountain loomed on the far side of town, faceless and void of detail, nothing but an ominous profile through the mist.

Sophie crossed the sidewalk and opened the door as slowly as she could.

A cluster of bells hanging from the inner handle jingled anyway.

Seymour didn't look back.

Aside from Seymour and an old man eating pie at a table against the opposite wall, the diner stood empty.

A jukebox in back played fifties rock-and-roll at an unobtrusive volume.

Two waitresses chatted at the counter, and one of them—a short blonde no more than twenty—glanced at Sophie and said, "Sit anywhere you like."

She slid into an empty booth just two down from Seymour's. Didn't like having her back to the door, but there was no way around it without facing the man.

He could have been asleep he sat so still, but his posture was rigid, on alert, staring straight ahead into nothing.

Sophie peeled the menu from the table and opened it more out of habit than hunger.

The usual suspects: variations of eggs and fried meat, a few burgers, a suspicious Cobb salad.

She looked out the window.

The rain had picked up.

At the intersection, a traffic light flashed red to green, but the road was empty.

"Have you decided?"

Sophie turned to find the young waitress standing poised with pad and pencil. She wore her hair in an impossibly tight ponytail, the brown of her roots clinging for dear life.

"Just a coffee."

"That's it?" she grieved.

"That's it."

The waitress let her pad drop, cocked her head, and popped a smile so enormous it seemed to exceed the square footage of her face.

"Haven't seen you here before. Your first time?"

Sophie's eyes cut to Seymour two booths up.

"Just passing through. Needed a caffeine fix."

"Oh? Where you headed?"

The question boomed in the silence of the diner as if it had been channeled through a PA system.

"Portland."

"Business or—"

"Just visiting family."

The waitress held her smile, as if Sophie's explanation needed more explanation and she had all the time in the world to wait for the rest of the story.

Across the diner, the old man looked up from his pie.

This line of questioning needed to end. Now.

"You know what, Jenny?" Sophie said, squinting at her nametag, "I think I will have a slice of your pie."

The waitress somehow squeezed out more smile.

"Good choice. Best in the state. Coffee and pie coming right up."

As Jenny headed off toward the counter, Sophie kept thinking that at any moment Seymour would suddenly turn and make her.

The waitress returned with a steaming carafe, a mug, and a slice of cherry pie.

She set everything down in front of Sophie.

Poured.

"Anything else, ma'am?"

Ma'am?

"No thanks."

"Enjoy."

Jenny the waitress moved on to Seymour's booth.

Sophie straightened in her seat.

The waitress smiled down at Seymour, but the speed at which it vanished indicated there was zero warmth returned from the customer.

"You haven't touched your coffee, sir. Can I get you something else?"

Seymour lifted his coffee and polished it off in one uninterrupted tilting of the mug.

He set it down empty on the table and looked up at the waitress.

"The coffee is excellent."

"Um, would you like some more?"

"Yes."

She filled his mug from the carafe.

"Anything else?"

"No."

Sophie pulled out her phone and tapped out three texts to Dobbs.

trailed BS to swartwoods diner in north bend

he's just sitting here being creepy

still no sign of talbert?

...

Sophie watched a dreary afternoon unspool through the windows. Customers came, left.

Three times she pulled out the receipt with Seymour's sketch, drawn to it on some frequency she couldn't name.

The weather cleared and rolled in again.

Still, she could count the number of cars that drove by on both hands.

In the beginning, the waitress had come by every ten minutes or so, pushing the menu, pushing more coffee, more pie. But after two hours, she was completely ignoring both Sophie and Seymour.

The sun dipped behind the mountains.

Darkness roused the streetlights, the empty intersection now washed in yellow light that made the wet pavement glisten.

A neon beer sign blinked to life in the window of a bar across the street.

Fifteen minutes crawled by.

Not a soul darkened its doorstep.

Happy hour on Friday night in North Bend.

And still, Seymour hadn't moved. Not to use the restroom. Or stretch his legs. Not even to readjust his weight on the hard plastic bench that had kept one or both of Sophie's legs in a perpetual state of pins and needles.

Out of sheer boredom, Sophie had blazed through four cups of coffee, a mistake she'd been paying the price for over the last hour as she watched customers enter the bathroom at the back of the diner and exit moments later with what she perceived to be orgasmic relief across their faces.

By 5:55 p.m., she couldn't hold it anymore.

Rising, she walked unsteadily down the aisle of window-adjacent booths, passing Seymour without acknowledgment or glance, and made a beeline for the doors at the back of the restaurant.

It was the first time she'd used her legs in over three hours, and they felt like they belonged to someone else.

She gave one quick look back at Seymour before disappearing into the women's restroom.

The desperation in her bladder crescendoed as she burst through the stall door and raced to unbuckle her belt.

Epic relief.

So intense it gave her chills.

She washed up quickly, uncomfortable with leaving Seymour out of sight, even for a minute.

She turned off the tap and looked around, hands dripping.

No paper towels.

No electric dryer.

Of course.

She shook them dry, finishing the job on the sides of her pants.

When she opened the door, her stomach clenched.

Three men now occupied Seymour's booth.

Sophie rebooted, pushed through the shock, and walked right past them, digging the phone out of her purse as she eased back into her booth.

Fired off a new text to Dobbs.

> still here ... two other men just showed up ... come now

She glanced out her window, saw a black van that hadn't been there before she'd left for the bathroom.

> possibly arrived in black GMC savana

Jenny the waitress sidled up to Seymour's booth, all smiles again.
"Can I get you gentlemen something to drink?"
"Coffee."
"Coffee."
"More coffee."
"Sure thing."
Sophie slid across the bench seat to get a look at the faces of the new arrivals.
One she didn't recognize—a man in his mid-fifties, ruggedly handsome, with wavy, graying curls that he kept swept back from his face.
The second was Barry Talbert, her other MIA.
Sophie's pulse rate doubled.
Talbert was the youngest of the trio—early forties if she had to guess. He wore a crisp, pinstripe button-down, open at the collar. Hair pushed back and cemented in place with plenty of product. At least two days' worth of stubble coming in.
Another text.

> talbert just walked in with some other guy

Both Talbert and Rugged-Handsome exuded that same trance-like intensity.
No one spoke.
A minute into the silence, Talbert broke his thousand-yard stare, looked at Seymour, shook his head, and looked away again, as if he'd been offered something and were politely refusing it.
The waitress returned with two coffee mugs and a carafe.

"Anyone interested in dinner?"

Seymour seemed to speak for everyone. "No, we're fine."

When the waitress was out of earshot, Talbert said, "We have the van."

Seymour nodded.

Talbert said, "Any word from him?"

"It hasn't happened yet."

Silence again.

Seymour looked at Talbert as if he'd spoken. He reached over and grabbed a plastic tub of creamer from a pile that filled a porcelain bowl beside the other condiments. Rolled it across the table to him.

Talbert tore off the seal and dumped the creamer into his coffee.

For a moment, he stared down into the cup, mesmerized, as if the swirls of cream were revealing the mysteries of the universe.

Rugged-Handsome said, "The children are there."

"Full house," Seymour said.

"He looks a lot like him."

"So does she," Talbert said without looking up.

The other two nodded in agreement.

"Won't be long now," Seymour said.

Silence descended on their booth again.

Sophie reeled.

On those rare occasions when she escaped the precinct for lunch hour, she liked to head downtown to Lola on Fourth and Virginia. She'd always take a book, intending to read, but inevitably she'd never even power it on. Instead, she'd sit alone, eating and soaking up fragments of conversation from the pleasant noise of the restaurant, reassembling them as best she could into a picture of the lives and stories of the people all around her. She was good at it too. Easy work for a detective and aspiring novelist.

But that particular aptitude was failing her at the moment.

It was different with Seymour, Talbert, and Rugged-Handsome.

Eavesdropping on their conversation was like trying to make sense of a dream. Like reading a code without the cipher. The words were plain enough, but they were fragments of a larger picture that she couldn't even begin to guess at.

She dug out her phone and sent another text to Dobbs.

something about to happen ... how far?

Ten seconds later, her screen illuminated.

10 min

She set the phone on the table.
Seymour straightened.
So did Sophie.
His head ticked to the left, as imperceptibly as the twitch of the minute hand, but she caught it.
The other two men watched him, something like wonder and fear exploding in their eyes.
Sophie thumbed off the brass snap that secured her Glock in the holster.
"The fourth?" Talbert said.
Seymour nodded. "He just arrived."

Chapter 22

Grant had just thrown up for the third time in the last hour, and he was still hunched over the toilet in the downstairs bathroom, gasping for breath while Paige patted his back.

"You're going to feel better soon," she said. "I promise."

Grant wiped his mouth as an intense shiver wracked his body.

"How long until your client—"

"Anytime."

"You ready?"

"Yes."

She looked the part at least, having changed back into her kimono.

"Got your phone set up?" he asked.

"I didn't want to go in there alone. I'll do it when I take Steve up."

"You be careful. Guy could flip out he catches you trying to record him."

"I will be."

Grant struggled onto his feet and flushed the toilet. The spinning of the water made him queasy all over again. He ran the tap, bent down, rinsed and spit until his mouth no longer burned with bile.

Already, it was dark outside and even darker in the brownstone. By the illumination of the candle on the sink, Grant studied his reflection in the mirror. The soft light should have knocked off ten years, but instead he looked worse—pallid and sweat-glazed and thinner.

Eyes as dark as pits.

The headache raged on—felt like his frontal lobe had been dropped in a food processor.

"What time is it, Paige?"

"Six fifteen."

Through the pain and the fog, Grant registered the distant, manic anthem of an alarm, although it took him a minute to land upon the crisis that had triggered it.

He staggered out of the bathroom and into the kitchen, steadying himself against the island where his phone waited. There were candles everywhere—in the living room, dining room, at least a half dozen casting a flickering warmth across the kitchen.

"Stu was supposed to call me fifteen minutes ago," he said, picking it up.

He held the power button down for several seconds.

Nothing happened.

He tried again, pressing harder and longer, his thumbnail blanching from the pressure.

Might as well have been trying to power up a brick.

He finally dropped the phone and put his head on the counter, the chill of the tile providing the briefest flash of relief.

"Grant, what's wrong?"

"Battery's dead."

"So your friend can't call you?"

"Right."

"Just use my phone."

"I don't know his number off the top of my head, and he's not on the Internet."

"So what do we do?"

Grant looked up from the counter.

It felt like someone was prodding around in his head with a screwdriver.

"I don't know. That was our best chance."

Paige came over, laid a cool hand on the back of his neck.

"We're gonna get through this," she said.

A noise reverberated down the hallway—someone pounding on the front door. It seemed to shake the entire building.

"That would be Steve," Paige said.

Grant choked down the despair, the exhaustion, the agony.

No time for pain.

He pulled himself up.

"I'll be in the closet by the bar."

Chapter 23

Sophie nearly jumped out of the booth when her cell began to vibrate.

She glanced down at the caller ID—*Stu Frank*.

It took her a moment to place the name—a semi-shady private investigator she and Grant had used once or twice. If she remembered correctly, Stu was ex-law enforcement. Six or seven years ago, he'd been thrown under the bus over a scandal involving several detectives and an ill-advised beat down of an errant CI. Even during their limited contact, she'd hated working with him. The man radiated an intense skin-crawling aura.

What the hell could you possibly want?

She answered quietly with, "Really not a good time, Stu."

"I've got something for Grant, but I can't get a hold of him."

"I'm his partner, not his mother."

"Be that as it may, you're still the closest thing to a mother he's got. Now I have some info on this crazy-urgent request he hit me with this afternoon. I've been trying to call him, but he's not picking up."

She felt her interest prickling.

Said, "When did he say he needed this by?"

"Two minutes ago. Six p.m. He was adamant. I've called five times, and it's been straight to voice mail. This house got something to do with a hot case or what?"

She didn't know how to answer that, so she just said, "Yeah."

"Is Grant with you?"

"No, but I'm going to see him later."

Through the window, Sophie watched the headlights of what looked like a Crown Vic whip into the parking space beside the black van.

"What do you want me to do with this file, Sophie?"

She opened her purse, dug out her wallet, threw a ten spot on the table.

"Where are you right now, Stu?"

"Cafe Vita in The Hill."

She slid out of the booth.

"I'll meet you there in twenty," she said.

She met Dobbs at the entrance.

"Outside, Art."

They stood in the drizzle.

"What's the word, Sophie?"

Art didn't exactly look like a law enforcement badass with his receding hairline and burgeoning paunch, but the threadbare JCPenney suit belied a damn good shot and one of the best detectives Sophie had ever worked with.

"Talbert, Seymour, and a John Doe are seated at one of the booths by the window. Stay on them."

"You're leaving?"

"I just got a call about Grant."

"I thought he was sick."

"I'm not so sure."

"He in trouble?"

"I don't know yet. I'll call you."

"I had a reservation at Canlis tonight for me and the wife."

Sophie was already moving across the sidewalk toward her TrailBlazer.

"I owe you one," she said over her shoulder.

"Yeah you do."

"Text me when they move. I'll be in the city."

Chapter 24

Grant stumbled over to the closet, slipped inside, and pulled the door closed after him.

He sat on the floor.

Drew his knees into his chest.

Buried his head in his hands.

The pain was operatic—audible through the silence like a throbbing timpani drum. He wondered how Paige had held out for three days by herself. In the years they'd been estranged, the memory of his little sister had been replaced by the image of the addict, the fuck-up, and now, the prostitute. It was easy to forget the little girl who would quietly stroke his hair when the tears he had fought back during the day finally arrived in the middle of the night. Those muffled sobs he'd tried to stifle with a pillow. She was stronger than he would ever be.

Now, with his head splitting apart in the darkness, he wished—as he had so many times before—that he could find some of her strength in himself. But he had never been the brave one.

Grant heard the front door close, followed by low voices in the foyer. Reaching up, he gently twisted the knob and nudged the closet door open a quarter of an inch.

He caught a twinkle of candlelight through the crack, and then Paige's voice.

"I'm so glad you came, Steve."

"What's with all the candles?"

"You don't like them?"

"I can't tell if it's romantic or if you're about to subject me to some Satanic ritual sacrifice."

Paige laughed, but Grant could tell it wasn't the genuine article—too quick, too high, definitely forced.

"The boring truth," she said, "is that the power went out."

"Bummer."

Their voices seemed to occupy the same airspace. Grant imagined her arms wrapped around the man's neck.

"I'm glad you called," the man said. "Thought you might have forgotten about me."

"Never."

Silence, and then the phlegmy slurp of kissing.

Grant grimaced.

"You feeling all right?" the man asked. "You look tired."

"Nothing you can't fix. Get us a drink?"

"Please."

Footsteps plodded toward the closet, and in the soft candlelight, Grant watched his sister approach the wet bar.

For a split second, her eyes shot to the crack between door and doorframe.

"Power's been out since last night," she said, "so no rocks." She grabbed a half-empty bottle.

I could use a hit of that right about now.

"Neat's the only way I drink," the man said as he emerged from the shadows and slid his arms around Paige's waist from behind. "I thought you'd remember that."

Steve wasn't at all what he had expected. He'd been prepared for another Jude—tall, perfect hair, chiseled everything. But Steve was shorter than Paige. As he sidled up behind her, the profile of his face met the slope of her neck like a puzzle piece, the top of his head stopping a full four inches below her own. He was thirty-five or forty pounds overweight and the dome of his hairless skull shone like polished marble in the candlelight. Physically at least, Steve was a completely unremarkable specimen. Grant couldn't decide if it made him feel better or worse to know that not all of Paige's clients were demigods.

Paige poured two glasses of scotch and turned to Steve.

"Should we take this upstairs?" she asked.

"You read my mind."

Grant listened to their footsteps trail away into the foyer.

The stairs creaked as they climbed.

Only when they'd reached the second floor did Grant ease the closet door open and step out.

The ceiling creaked above him.

He pictured Steve and Paige heading down the hall toward her bedroom.

Their footfalls stopped. The bedroom door groaned open.

As if on cue, his ears popped—like rolling down the windows in a speeding car.

Grant exhaled.

He strained to listen, but there was nothing else to hear.

Moving around to the wet bar, Grant lifted the best thing he saw—a twenty-five year Highland Park—and poured into a rocks glass.

Shot it.

The whiskey dumping into his empty stomach like a fistful of lava.

He poured another, swirled it.

No plans of stopping until the world lost its hard edge.

Grant raised the glass in the air before him.

"A toast," he said, "to shit."

There was a knock at the front door.

For a moment, he wrote it off as a phantom sound. A glitch in his fracturing mind. He waited for confirmation, willing the silence to continue.

Another knock, this time harder.

He set the glass on the bar and made his way into the foyer, careful to stay clear of the windows that faced the street.

Without power, the intercom and camera were useless.

He pressed up against the door, eye to the peephole.

Sophie stared back at him.

He blinked.

Still there.

He clawed his way through the pain and tried to think.

What are you doing here?

What are you doing here?

What are you—

Stu.

That was the only conceivable way. The PI had tried to call at six p.m. like Grant had insisted . But his phone was dead. So naturally, Stu called his partner.

A flare of heat rushed through his face—anger at himself. At his shortsighted plan. He should've seen this possible outcome a mile away. You always plan for the worst case scenario. Should've told Stu this research was for something on the side. Something no other person in the world—least of all his partner—needed to know about.

Goddamnit.

Sophie pounded on the door again.

Grant played the scene forward.

Open it?

What would he possibly say to her? Maybe on his best day—when a world-class migraine hadn't liquefied his brain and he actually had time to prepare—maybe then he'd have a *chance* at talking his way out of this. At assuaging whatever concerns she had and convincing her to leave without suspicion. But not in his current condition. Sophie would see through the lies before they even left his mouth. Hell, all she'd have to do was take one look at his sunken eyes and know he'd gotten himself into something bad.

So wait her out.

She knocked again, and he saw her gauzy silhouette lean into the curtained window frame to the right of the door. He knew she couldn't see inside, but still he didn't dare move from his spot behind the door.

Sure this is the right play? To just let her leave and bring back a search warrant?

Yes. Let her go. She'll be back, no doubt, but Steve will be gone and we'll have bought a little time to figure something out.

Sophie appeared in the peephole again. She looked left and then right. Grant's heart nearly exploded when the doorknob rattled. Thank God it was locked. Finally, she turned away and headed back down the steps.

Grant shut his eyes.

Lines of sweat meandered down the sides of his face and through the stubble of his beard.

He knew the pain would return, but for the moment, he basked in the numbing effect of the adrenaline rush that was ripping through his system.

If nothing else, he'd bought them a few hours.

Use it wisely.

Grant trudged back over to the bar and picked up the shot of Highland.

He swirled the amber liquid, tried to appreciate its color, its nose, but the whiskey was no match for the shitstorm on the horizon.

He downed it.

Shouldn't have, but the best detective in town had just knocked on their door. He and Paige were going to have to deal with Don in the upstairs bathroom.

They were going to have to deal with a lot of things.

And fast.

Somewhere in the house, glass shattered. His first thought was *Paige*, but the sound hadn't come from upstairs.

He stumbled into the kitchen.

Now it sounded like shards of glass were falling onto concrete or stone.

More noise erupted—furniture overturning.

Grant stood facing a door beside the hallway, which based upon its alignment under the staircase, he figured led down into the basement.

As if in confirmation, footfalls began clomping up a set of stairs on the other side.

He staggered back, ducked around the kitchen island, and lowered himself out of sight.

The basement door swung open so slowly he could swear he heard the scraping of each individual grain of rust on the hinges.

Grant peered around the corner of the island.

Knew it was Sophie before he saw her.

Black pantsuit over a cobalt blouse that fit her like a Bond girl.

Gun drawn and everything.

"Seattle Police. Anyone here?"

The heels of Sophie's platform boots knocked against the hardwood floor. He knew he should speak up, but he couldn't bring himself to push out that first word.

She turned and started down the hallway, her back to him.

Now.

Now.

Now.

"Sophie," he whispered.

She stopped, spun, gun sighting down the kitchen. "Who's there?"

"It's Grant."

"Where are you?"

"Behind the island. I'm standing up. You can put your gun away, or at least not shoot me."

He struggled slowly onto his feet.

Sophie was barely visible in the gloom of the hallway. She stepped back into the candlelit kitchen.

"What are you doing here?" she asked.

"Bad lead, long story. How'd you find me?"

She moved in closer toward the island.

"Are we safe here?" she asked.

"Yeah, it's just us."

She holstered her Glock. "What are you doing here, Grant?"

"I don't want you to get mad—"

"I'm not mad. I'm confused."

"I have a contact at the Four Seasons."

"Okay."

"He's a concierge. I went to him with what we had on our Facebook girls. He pointed me here."

"To this brownstone?"

"Yes. He told me it was a high-end brothel."

"So the food poisoning ..."

"I'm sorry."

"And you felt the need to keep this from me why?"

"Nothing I'm proud of."

"I don't even know what that means."

"I've used this concierge before."

"As an informant?"

"No."

"Oh." Sophie looked at the countertop, then back at Grant. "And you thought I might, what? Judge you? Because that's the kind of person you know me to be?"

"I don't know what I thought. That was a long time ago, when I was in a really bad place. But still ... I was embarrassed. Didn't want you to find out. And besides, this isn't exactly by the book."

"No shit. Who lives here?"

"One of our Facebook girls used to. This was her last known."

Sophie leaned forward, took in a long breath.

"So who lives here now?"

"Some U-Dub trust funder. Definitely *not* a person of interest."

"Did you not hear me knocking on the door five minutes ago?"

"I was upstairs."

Sophie nodded. "What's the current tenant's name?"

"Heidi Spiegel."

"She here? I'd love to meet Ms. Spiegel."

It was faint—practically undetectable—but Grant heard the rhythmic creak of Sophie's bed springs starting up on the second floor.

"She's gone," Grant said. "I parked on the street. Came in when I saw her leave."

"Just let yourself in, huh?"

"Door wasn't locked."

"Interesting choice."

"Says the detective who broke in through the basement."

"I was worried about you, Grant. I thought you were in some kind of trouble."

"I'm fine."

"Thrilled to hear it. What's with all the candles?"

Grant walked over to a light switch beside the sink, gave it a few flips.

"No power," he said.

"Strange that Ms. Spiegel would just leave all these candles burning."

"Probably means she didn't plan on being gone long. We should get out of here."

"You been drinking?" Sophie asked. "You smell like booze."

What could he do? Deny?

"I had a whiskey at the hotel before I rolled up here. You have an issue with that?"

Sophie smiled a smile that wasn't. She stared Grant down across the island and shook her head.

"What?" Grant said.

"You are so full of shit it's not even funny."

"What are you talking about?"

"Has one thing you've said to me in the last three minutes even entered the same ballpark as the truth?"

"Yeah. Everything."

"Look at you. What are you wearing? Jeans and a T-shirt?"

My real clothes are covered in the blood of Don McFee who's at this moment passing through rigor mortis in a room directly above our heads because of something I still don't understand. What if I laid that *on you, partner? Then what?*

Grant's headache and nausea vanished. He felt suddenly perfect, like someone had thrown a switch or hit him with a beautiful morphine push. He straightened, reevaluating everything absent the distraction of agony.

"You're not even wearing shoes, Grant."

Fair point.

"Where's your gun? Where's your shield?"

"In my car."

"You wanna tell me what's really going on here?"

"I just did."

"No, you just lied to me. For the second time today."

"Sophie—"

Heavy footsteps thumped above them on the second floor.

Sophie cocked her head. "Thought you said we were alone."

"Listen to me."

She turned and started down the hallway as the footfalls reached the top of the stairs.

"Sophie, come back here."

They began their descent.

Grant moved around the island and followed Sophie down the hall.

By the time he reached her at the foyer, Steve Vincent was five steps from the bottom of the staircase and progressing at a steady, unhurried pace toward the front door, the same incomprehensible vacancy in his eyes that Grant had seen in Jude's. Steve wore pants and shoes, but his shirt, coat, and tie he carried in a bundle under his left arm.

Sophie said, "Sir, do you live here?"

Steve reached the foyer and walked past them to the front door.

"Excuse me, sir, I just asked you a question."

The man turned the two deadbolts and slung back the chain.

"Sir! Seattle Po—"

Grant said, "Let him go."

Steve opened the door, disappeared outside.

Sophie looked at Grant.

"Who was that?"

Where to begin?

Sophie looked up the staircase. She started toward it, but Grant stepped into her path.

"That's not a good idea," he said.

The intensity in her eyes belied a card he'd never seen her play—fear.

"What have you gotten yourself into, Grant?"

Where to even begin?

"Get out of my way," she said.

"I can't let you go up there."

"Grant?" From upstairs, his sister called his name.

"Who's that?" Sophie asked.

His eyes flashed to her belt.

Back to her face.

At least he could think again.

"Grant!"

"Who's calling you, Grant?"

With his arms already at his sides, Grant eased his left hand forward and went for it—flicked open the brass snap on Sophie's belt and snatched her handcuffs before she had a chance to react.

He locked a bracelet around her left wrist as her right hand shot into her jacket.

Glimpsed the black composite stock of her G22 as she tore it out of the holster.

He slapped the barrel, the Glock ripping out of Sophie's grasp and arcing toward the living room.

It struck the hardwood and slid across the floor as Grant jerked the handcuffs toward the banister and locked the other bracelet around a baluster.

It came with a vengeance—Sophie swinging with her free right arm, her fist slamming into Grant's jaw with enough force to turn his head and kill the lights.

Grant came to on his back at the foot of the stairs, sat up punch drunk to the sound of keys clinking together.

He scrambled to his feet and lunged at Sophie, snagging the key chain out of her grasp and ducking as her fingernails raked at his face.

Grant stumbled back as she pulled against the balustrade.

The front door to the brownstone stood wide open.

He crossed the foyer and closed it, locked back the deadbolts and rehung the chain.

"The fuck is wrong with you?" Sophie screamed.

His jaw throbbed, hot to the touch. Bruised but not broken.

"I'm sorry," he said.

One of the steps near the top of the staircase creaked. Grant looked up, saw the shape of his sister descending through the darkness.

She stopped halfway to the bottom and eased down onto a step.

"What's going on, Grant?"

"We had a visitor while you were upstairs."

"Who you've handcuffed to the banister?"

"Paige, meet Sophie. My partner."

Paige rested her forehead against her knees and said, "Oh God."

"Sophie, meet Paige. My sister."

Sophie glared up the staircase, and then back at Grant.

He said, "Paige, we need to talk. Could you come join me in the kitchen please?" And then to Sophie. "Give me your purse."

She wiped the mascara-stained tears from her cheeks and threw it at him.

"I hate this," Grant said.

He unzipped her handbag and fished out her phone. Powered it off, slid it into the side pocket of his jeans.

He set the purse on the first step and looked at his partner, asked, "Who else knows that you came here?"

Paige walked past Sophie and Grant and started down the hallway toward the kitchen.

"Fuck you."

"Sophie, I will explain everything to you. I promise. But right now, I need to know if more people are coming. For all of our safety."

She blinked through a sheet of tears that glistened in the candlelight and said at barely a whisper, "Just me."

"How's the hand? You didn't break it hitting me, did you?"

"No."

"The cuffs all right? Too tight?"

She shook her head.

Grant paused at the banister on his way down the hall and tested the bracelet around Sophie's left wrist and the bracelet around the balustrade.

Chapter 25

Paige stood waiting for him at the kitchen island, her face grim in the candlelight.

"How bad is this?" she asked.

"We need to leave."

"And how are we supposed to do that?"

"I don't know, but more people will come."

"From your work?"

"Yes."

"What's going to happen when they ..." She cut her eyes toward the ceiling.

"Nothing good."

"Your face is swollen."

"She hit me." Grant glanced back down the hallway. "I should talk to her."

"About what?"

"Make her understand what's—"

"No."

"No?"

"Why would you tell her about any of this?"

"Does it not look bad enough already? I just handcuffed my own partner to a staircase and took her gun."

"How'd she even find you?"

"The private investigator I called this afternoon. My phone died, he couldn't reach me, so he called her."

"Does this mean she talked to your PI?"

"I would assume."

"So maybe she has some info on the house."

"I'll find out. I'm going to tell her everything, Paige."

"Why would you do that?"

"Because maybe she believes me, and then it's three of us against whatever's upstairs."

"You didn't believe me until you saw your friend cut his neck open with a piece of glass."

"Maybe you're right. Maybe she won't believe me. But she will listen."

Grant sat down a foot outside of Sophie's reach.

She glared at him, dark eyes ablaze with equal parts sadness, anger, and fear. In the thousands of hours they'd spent together, he'd never seen this look before. A new level of intimacy reached under the worst possible conditions. It felt unnatural, impossible that he might be the object of that intensity. That *he* had hurt her. In the back of his mind, he'd always thought it would be the other way around.

"I need you to do something, Sophie."

With her free hand, she pushed her straight black hair out of her face. "What?"

"Try and remember what it felt like to trust me."

"Are you joking?"

"Three months ago, when you had your biopsy—"

"Don't do that."

"Hear me out. You know I would have been sitting in that waiting room when you came out, whether you asked me to be there or not."

Grant thought he saw the hardness in her eyes give just a little.

He went on, "Now imagine the kind of situation the guy sitting in that doctor's office would have to be in to physically disarm you and chain you to a banister. Imagine how scared out of his mind he'd have to be."

"I can't if you don't tell me."

"I'm going to. And I hope you think about all the things you love, or used to love, about me. I hope you'll give me the benefit of all the doubts you have."

"Why should I?"

"Because no one in their right mind would believe what I'm about to tell you."

It was raining again. Grant could hear it pattering on the windows. A good, rich smell wafted in from the kitchen. The soft crackle of browning butter. Paige making grilled cheese sandwiches, he hoped.

The modest heat of the day had fled and a damp, merciless chill had begun to overtake the brownstone.

"Those Facebook profiles you sent me last night?"

"Yeah?"

"One of them was just a pair of eyes, but I recognized them. They were my sister's. What I said about the concierge was true. He told me about this place. I showed up last night, and sure enough, Paige was living here."

"Your sister, the one you hadn't seen in years, is living in Queen Anne and working as a prostitute?"

Grant nodded. "Maybe you can understand why I came here alone."

"I'll give you that."

"She let me in, and right off, I noticed she didn't look well. Strung out, I figured. She's always struggled with addiction, so I've seen it before. But nothing like this. She looked emaciated. Pale as a ghost."

"You should've called me."

"Be glad I didn't."

"Why?"

Grant glanced up the staircase.

His stomach churned.

"I need to show you something. If I uncuff you, am I going to regret it?"

"No."

Grant walked into the living room, grabbed the flashlight from the coffee table, and then retrieved Sophie's Glock from beneath a tufted wingback chair that sat in the corner. He pocketed the magazine, racked the slide, and caught the semi-jacketed .40 cal hollowpoint in midair.

"You think I'd shoot you?" she asked.

"You ever think I'd cuff you to a banister?"

Grant dug her keys out of his pocket as he walked back over to the stairs. Unlocking the bracelet from the balustrade, he cuffed it around his own wrist and helped Sophie onto her feet.

"Can I see your hand?" he asked.

She held it up, the swelling already begun along the ring and pinkie fingers below the knuckles, Sophie's light brown skin flashing the darkening blush of a bruise.

"Next time you hit someone," Grant said, "keep your fist closed."

"Your jaw's an asshole," she said.

"You hit like a girl." He motioned toward the steps. "We're headed up."

"Why?"

"To show you something."

"Can't you just tell me?"

"Remember what they say about seeing?"

"No."

"It's believing."

They climbed in tandem, Grant's right hand bound to Sophie's left. Halfway up, they lost the morsels of light from the candles down below. Grant switched on the flashlight, its beam striking the landing above them with a circle of illumination that seemed much weaker than the last time he'd used it.

He was suddenly aware of the shudder of his heart, like something shaking manically inside his chest.

"What's wrong?" Sophie asked.

"I don't like it up here."

They reached the second floor and Grant led them to the foot of the corridor that accessed Paige's bedroom.

He passed the beam over the table, the lamp, the peeling wallpaper.

"What are we doing up here?" Sophie asked.

Grant shone his flashlight on the bedroom door.

Still closed.

"We're almost there," he said.

They moved down the corridor. As they neared Paige's room, Grant felt himself struggling against the same fear he'd known as a child—staring down the hall from his bedroom in the middle of the night, weighing his thirst for a drink of water from the kitchen against the knowledge that he'd have to walk past the yawning black mouth of the bathroom to get it.

As they passed Paige's door, Grant felt that magnetic pull he'd dreamt of.

A burning desire crystallized in the back of his mind which contained all the fatal allure of a suicidal question ...

What would the barrel of this gun taste like?
What would it feel like to jump?
What if I stepped in front of that bus?
What if I just opened the door?

It would be the simplest action, one he'd done tens of thousands of times in his life.

Just turn the knob and push.

"Grant, you okay?"

He realized he'd stopped walking.

Was standing with the tip of his nose several inches from Paige's door, his flashlight pointed at the carpet.

"Yeah, this way," he said, pulling himself away from the door.

They moved together to the end of the hall.

Turning the corner, they came to the guestroom.

Grant stopped at the closed door.

"What now?" Sophie asked.

In all the turmoil, Grant realized he'd overlooked the fact that this wasn't just going to shock Sophie, it was going to hurt her as much as it had hurt him. She'd known Don too, and not only in a professional capacity. During her cancer scare, Don had availed himself to her. His wife had gone through a similar ordeal the year before. His insight, coupled with an uncanny ability to demystify fear and help people stare it right in the face, had gone a long way toward getting Sophie through those excruciating days between the biopsy and the results. He had become as much a fixture in her life as he had been in Grant's. Don was a healer, and he had touched them both in their darkest moments.

"Instead of calling you last night," Grant said, "I called Don. He came over, tried to talk to Paige. She was acting crazy. Saying there was something upstairs in her bedroom. That she couldn't leave the house. I thought she was psychotic."

Grant opened the door.

"Don offered to come upstairs and walk through her bedroom. Prove to her there was nothing strange going on. That it was all in her mind."

"Is this her bedroom?" Sophie asked.

"No. This is where I found Don. After he'd been inside her bedroom."

"What do you mean 'found him?' Is Don okay?"

"No."

She snatched the flashlight out of his hand and started into the guestroom.

"Sophie, it's not pretty."

She was already crying. "I've seen not pretty before."

"But anyone you loved?"

She was shining the light all over the room.

"Where?" she asked.

"Bathroom."

She dragged Grant toward the doorway.

He didn't want to go through it again. Once in real life, once in a dream—that was all he had in him.

Sophie stopped.

Her shoulders sagged, and he heard the air go out of her, like she was deflating.

She leaned against the doorframe and put the light on Don.

She didn't make a sound.

In twenty-four hours, the nose of the room had changed markedly, like a wine opening up. Not exactly fetid, but rich and dank—the intensity of a greenhouse with a disturbing note of sweetness creeping in.

"Oh, Don."

"He broke the mirror and cut his own throat with a piece of glass," Grant said.

Under the fading illumination of the flashlight, the blood on the checkerboard tile looked as black as oil. It had lost its lustrous sheen, now dulled, congealed, and spiderwebbed with cracks like the surface of a four-hundred-year-old oil painting.

Even in the bad light, the changes in Don were evident. The skin of his face looked loose and waxy and drained of color save for a few dark spots where the blood had pooled underneath.

Sophie still hadn't taken her eyes off him.

She said, "He went into Paige's room. Then he came in here and killed himself. That's what you're saying happened."

"No, that's what happened."

"Have you called Rachel?"

"Not yet."

Sophie glared at him. "You've let her just wonder where her husband is for the last twenty-four hours?"

"And what would you have done?"

"She must be out of her mind by now. We have to call her."

"Are you crazy?"

"Are you?"

"And tell her what exactly? I still don't understand what's—"

"We have to bring some people in on this, Grant. Don't you think it's time for that? I mean, Jesus Christ, look at this."

He stepped back out of the doorway, dragging Sophie along.

Said, "We don't know what we're dealing with yet."

"All the more reason."

"You don't understand. When people set foot in this house, it changes them."

"What are you talking about?"

"Seymour? He was a client of my sister's. He came here just before he disappeared."

"Seriously?"

"Something happened to him in Paige's room. You obviously saw the effect it had."

"Grant—"

"Barry Talbert too. He was here this week. And another man came last night. Went up with Paige into her bedroom, and then walked out like a goddamn zombie. Just like the man you saw twenty minutes ago."

"This man last night … did he have wavy gray hair? Strong build? An inch or two over six feet?"

"Yeah, his name is Jude Grazer. He's a doctor. How do you know about him?"

"When Stu called me, I was at this little diner in North Bend watching Grazer, Talbert, and Seymour having coffee in one of the booths."

Grant felt a coldness move down the center of his back. He said, "These men were there *together*?"

"Yep."

"Doing what?"

"No idea. But they were acting very strange."

"What were they talking about?"

"Nothing that came close to making sense."

"Why would they be together? There's no connection between Seymour and Talbert."

"Um … your sister?"

"And you just left them?"

"Only when I thought you might be in trouble. But Art took my place. He's there now, won't let them out of his sight."

Grant sat down on the end of the bed.

"What do you think would happen, Sophie, if I called in the cavalry right now?"

"The cavalry would come."

"And then what? When I told them this crazy story I just told you. When I showed them Don. When you told them how I'd disarmed you and cuffed you to a staircase, and then to me?" He held up their chained wrists. "How exactly would all of that go over?"

Sophie stared at the floor.

Grant said, "Interrogation. Psyche eval. Suspect. And what would happen to my sister?"

"I respect you, Grant. You know that. And so do a lot of other people. Sure. There'd be questions—"

"That I don't have answers to. I can't explain it. Not any of it. And on top of that, I can't leave this house."

"What do you mean you can't leave?"

"I can't physically leave this house. It has some kind of power over me. I tried last night after what happened to Don. When I got to the bottom of the front porch steps, this pain hit me. I threw up. My head felt like someone was beating me with a baseball bat. I would've died. The only relief was crawling back inside."

"I don't even know how to respond to that, Grant."

"You think I don't get that? That I don't fully understand that no one's going to believe me? And does that give you some small insight into the choices I've made during the last twenty-four hours?"

Sophie let out a slow, trembling breath. "I want to believe you, Grant. I do."

"I know. And I know it's hard."

"What exactly do you think is happening inside this house?"

"I have no idea."

"But it's focused in the vicinity of Paige's room?"

"Yes."

"Have you been in there?"

"No."

"Why?"

"Because everyone who sets foot inside comes out massively fucked."

"Except your sister."

"Did you just talk to Stu on the phone, or did you actually meet up with him before you came here?"

"I swung by the coffee shop. Why?"

"Didn't he have something for me?"

Sophie's eyes lost their thoughtful intensity. "Yeah, actually. A manila folder with some papers inside."

"Where is it?"

She hesitated. "In my car. What's in the folder? I haven't looked."

"Background history on this building. Prior residents. Ownership. Information that could possibly help us."

"Will you trust me to go out and get it and come right back?"

"Absolutely not. Sorry."

"It's okay, I wouldn't trust me either. It's not really in my car. I left it in the basement."

Chapter 26

The flashlight was practically worthless by the time Grant and Sophie reached the foyer. In the kitchen, Paige was flipping grilled cheese sandwiches at the stovetop. Grant swapped the flashlight for a pair of candles, and with his partner's wrist still chained to his, he pulled open the door to the basement.

The darkness hovered as thick as water, and it seemed to push back against the candlelight with a palpable force, limiting the sphere of illumination to only three or four feet. Clearly, the brownstone's recent renovation hadn't laid a finger on this creaky set of stairs, each step bowing under Grant's and Sophie's weight.

The fifteenth step spit them out at the bottom and Grant held the candle above his head to get a better look.

Walls of crumbling brick climbed to pairs of windows—two near the top of the wall that faced the street, two along the back wall. One of these had been shattered. Shards of glass glinted on the rough stone floor.

A hot water boiler occupied one gloomy corner.

An electrical box another.

These were the only things in the basement that looked to have been built in the last fifty years.

There were mouse droppings everywhere, and the cellar-temperature air reeked of must.

Grant moved past an upright piano against the wall that stood draped in cobwebs. A third of its yellowed ivory keys were missing.

They stopped at the remnants of a work bench underneath the broken window.

The right-hand side of its surface had been smashed in.

"This where you dropped down into the basement?" Grant asked.

"Yeah."

"Lucky you didn't break your legs."

"It was so dark, I couldn't tell how far the drop was."

Grant spotted a manila folder next to a rusty vise.

He set his candle down and opened it.

The first page was a spreadsheet entitled "Prior Tenants - 1990 to Present." It consisted of three columns (Name/Dates of Occupancy/Contact Info) and nine rows of names.

Under the spreadsheet were a number of reports, each individually stapled, and all spring-clamped together. Grant recognized Stu's handwriting on the first one.

6 out of 9 background checks, best I could do

Under the reports, he found one last item—a Residential Seller Property Disclosure. Across the top of this form, Stu had scrawled …

you owe me for this one

"This everything you asked Stu for?" Sophie said.

"Mostly." Grant leaned down, squinting at the poor photocopy of the property disclosure, but the light was bad. "I can't make any of this out." He reached into his pocket, pulled out Sophie's phone. It still had a three-quarter charge.

"Grant?"

"Yeah?"

"I can't believe I'm about to have a serious conversation about this, but I have an observation."

"Shoot."

"In thinking about Seymour and Talbert and the other men, there's a common theme which you appear to be overlooking."

"What's that?"

"Your sister."

"Meaning ..."

"This is *her* house. It's *her* bedroom they're all walking into and coming out like zombies. Or killing themselves."

"Point being?"

"You've got all this background info on the house—and that's useful—but are you sure you're not missing something that's staring you right in the face?"

"My sister is as much a victim—no, more so—than anyone. She's a wreck."

"But you have no idea what she's been doing for the last five years. I mean ... do you really even know her?"

"You're suggesting maybe Paige is the cause of all this?"

"I'm saying you seem to be looking everywhere but the obvious direction."

"She wasn't even in her room when Don went up there, Sophie. And you think she's somehow causing me to become violently ill when I step outside?"

"Who the hell knows? Assuming everything you've told me is true, we're dealing with a rulebook we've never seen before."

"Yes, she's an addict and a prostitute who has fucked her own life from every possible position, but that doesn't mean ... what are you saying exactly? That Paige has put a—for lack of a better word—*curse* on this house? On me? On everyone who walks in? Does this mean she's a witch? Come on."

"Remember what you wrote in my birthday card last month?"

"Sure."

"Say it back to me now."

He shook his head.

"You forgot."

"To Sophie. You're the best partner I've ever had because you see cases from angles I could never reach."

"Still believe that?" she asked.

"I do."

"Still want to dismiss my input so quickly?"

One of the steps creaked bloody murder.

Grant turned and stared at the shadow of his sister.

Paige stood as still as a statue halfway down the staircase.

"Everything okay?" Grant asked.

"Dinner's ready." Her voice was flat, void of emotion, unreadable.

"Great." He closed the manila folder and shelved it under his arm. "We're coming up."

Chapter 27

They sat at one end of the dining room table which Paige had forested in candles and cleared of the stacks of bills and junk mail. The grilled cheese sandwiches had been cut into triangles, and Paige ate quietly, eyes locked on her plate.

Grant and Sophie sat side-by-side, still cuffed together, perusing the contents of the folder. While Sophie skimmed the background reports, Grant studied the seller's property disclosure, a form required by state law to be completed by a seller of real property in a real estate transaction. The seller was obligated to disclose the presence of any structural, water, sewer/septic, common interest issues, and the like to the buyer.

Additionally, in most states, including Washington, material facts—anything that could influence a buyer's decision to purchase a home—had to be disclosed. This included a death on the property, particularly if violent or gruesome.

Grant flipped through the five-page document to one of the final questions:

Are there any other defects affecting the property known to the seller?

The "NO" box was checked.
Sophie said, "What's wrong? You just sighed."
"This disclosure form doesn't tell me anything."

"When did the property last change hands?"

Grant traced his finger to the bottom of the final page. The signature was indistinct, but he could read the date.

"Six years ago last March. Anything of note on your end?"

"There are actually seven background checks here. The first is on the current owner."

"What's their story?"

"Forty-nine year-old woman named Miranda Dupree. She's out of state. Lives in Sacramento. Nothing juicy. Just your plain-vanilla rich bitch. She owns a bunch of properties through an LLC. The tenant prior to Paige—Terry Flowers—has had two DUIs." She kept flipping. "Nothing else pops, but then again, Stu doesn't have access to the major league databases." Sophie dropped the reports on the table. "I don't even know what we're really looking for here, Grant."

"You and me both. That's how these things go, remember?"

"No, I've never had the pleasure of investigating a real haunted house before."

"Resume builder."

"Can't wait to update mine with all this new and relevant experience I'm gaining. Promotion for sure."

Grant grinned as he pulled out her phone and punched in a number.

"Who you calling?" Sophie asked.

"Station. You know who's on tonight?"

"Frances, I think."

"Good. She loves me."

Frances answered two rings later with a voice of smoke-laced apathy. "Investigations."

"Hi, Frances, it's your favorite detective. How are you?"

"Well, I'm here, so draw your own conclusion."

"Sophie and I are working on something and we're away from our laptops. Would you mind running an address through NCIC and ViCAP?"

"Sure. One second. Okay, hit me."

Grant stared across the table at his sister, looking for some reaction to what he was about to do, some sign of reassurance or disagreement. But she just chewed a bite of sandwich with complete absence, like she wasn't even seated at the same table.

"Grant? You there?"

Was it worth the risk? Putting the address out there?

"Grant? Did I lose you?"

He said, "Twenty-two Crockett Street."

He heard Frances typing.

"No love from ViCAP," she said. More typing. "No love from NCIC."

"Anything in our database? Maybe something that didn't get entered into NCIC?"

Frances's laugh sounded like rocks tumbling. "Like that could ever happen. Nothing in our database either."

"I'm going to e-mail you a photo of a spreadsheet with nine names. I want you to run them all and call me back on Sophie's cell with anything that pops."

"And you need this by ..."

"ASAFP."

"Oh good. I was going to spend the night playing Minesweeper, but this will be so much more fun."

"One more favor?"

"This what I get for being so accommodating?"

"Can we keep this request just between us?"

A long pause, and then: "You know every search gets logged automatically. Nothing I can do—"

"I understand that."

"Oh. You don't want me mentioning this in passing to the big man. That what you getting at?"

"Or anybody else."

"I won't bring it up—"

"Thank—"

"—unless someone brings it up to me. Then you on your own."

"All I ask. You're the best, Frances."

Grant snapped a photo of the spreadsheet and e-mailed it to Frances from Sophie's account.

He suddenly realized he was starving.

Bit a giant wedge out of one of the triangles.

"This is perfection," he said. "You okay, Paige?"

She looked up.

"I'm fine."

Sophie's phone vibrated—a text from Dobbs.

4th man just arrived ... how's grant?

Grant said, "Paige. Paige, look at me."

Paige raised her head.

"Your phone," Grant said. "Where is it?"

His sister's eyes looked distant and unfocused, even as she reached into the pocket of her kimono and held it up.

He said, "Sophie showed up, and I completely spaced it. We need to watch the video. The one you took of Steve."

Paige's eyes slammed back into the present.

"What video?" Sophie asked.

Paige said, "Whenever I take a man into my room, I always black out, and he's always gone when I wake up. With this last guy, Steve, I set up my phone and recorded us."

"Can I see it?" Grant said.

Paige shook her head. "I want to watch it first. Alone."

Chapter 28

Paige took her phone into the kitchen.

She was gone awhile.

Grant and Sophie stayed behind in the dining room.

While they waited, Grant tapped out a response to Dobbs's text:

grant's ok, send pic of new guy

Grant showed Sophie Dobbs's last text, said, "The fourth man has to be Steve. What do you make of it? Four men, none of whom—far as we know—have any personal connection beyond Paige. They go into her room. They disappear. Then they meet up. Why?"

"I wish you could've heard them talking. It was so strange."

"How so?"

"Like there was this whole other conversation happening below the surface, but they were only verbally expressing a fraction of it. I know it doesn't make sense."

"What does anymore?"

As Grant reached for his water glass, he heard Paige gasp in the kitchen.

"Paige?" he called out. "Everything okay?"

The door to the kitchen swung open.

Paige stood in the threshold. Even in the firelight, Grant could see that her face had lost all color, the tremors in her hands so violent they extended up into her shoulders.

He rose out of his seat and went to her.

Paige pushed her phone into his chest.

"What happened?" he asked.

She shook her head, eyes welling.

He took her by the arm and helped her into the chair.

Grant set the phone on the table and looked at Sophie, a knot tightening deep in his gut.

He turned the phone lengthwise, revived the touchscreen.

The video was cued.

Eleven minutes, forty-one seconds.

For a second, Paige's face fills the lens.
She pulls back, walks out of frame.
The view is level.
It shows a bedroom from a wide angle, three or four feet up off the floor.
Left-hand side of the frame: floor to ceiling drapes hide a window.
Right-hand side: double doors, presently closed, open into a closet.
The bed is centered almost perfectly in the shot.
Four posts reach for the ceiling.
The headboard is hidden behind a rampart of pillows.
Paige and Steve Vincent walk into frame, Paige holding his hand and guiding him toward the bed.
At least a dozen candles populate each bedside table, but still the light is poor and the picture grainy.
Paige unties the cloth belt and lets her kimono slide down her shoulders into a pool of silk around her feet.

Grant said, "How am I supposed to watch this?"

Sophie said, "Suck it up, you big baby."

"That's my sister."

Grant looked at his sister.

Paige was staring hard into the table like it was a visual sanctuary.

In that moment, he felt the strangest mix of anger and compassion toward her.

A conflicting yet simultaneous desire to hold her, to love her, to hurt her.

Vincent begins to moan.

Grant glanced down at the phone.

Took his eyes a moment to piece together what he saw.

The man is on his back, spread-eagle, with Paige between his legs, her head bobbing up and down.

Grant shut his eyes, and Paige must have caught a waft of the heat coming off him, because she said, "What did you think happened up in that room?"

"One thing to know. Another to see."

"Disapproval noted."

He forced himself to look back at the screen.

Vincent on top now. Missionary. Riding hard.

Sophie said, "Oh my God."

Grant's eyes cut to the closet doors, but he couldn't see that anything had changed.

"What? I don't see it."

She touched the screen.

At first, Grant didn't think it was real.

A trick of light and shadow perhaps.

A byproduct of the grainy picture.

The shadow keeps lengthening, a long, thin arm stretching out from the darkness under Paige's bed.

Vincent humps away unawares.

Faster and faster.

Getting loud.

He yells as he comes, an unmistakable component of rage in his voice that drowns out Paige.

And then ...

One minute, the man is on top of her, pounding away.

The next, Paige lies alone and motionless on the sheets as the last vestige of Vincent—his foot—slides under the bed.

For thirty seconds, the room is still.

Grant looked at Sophie, and then Paige.

"Did that just happen?"

"Yes," Sophie said.

"How is that—"

"I don't know."

He looked at Paige. She finally met his eyes. He said, "What happened?"

"I don't know."

"This isn't lightbulbs exploding or some unidentified illness. Something just dragged that man under your bed."

"I saw it."

"What is it?"

"I don't know!"

"It's in *your* room. Under *your* bed."

"Grant." Sophie nudged him and pointed at the screen.

A hand reaches out.

Then a head emerges.

Vincent wriggles out from under the bed and struggles slowly onto his feet.

For what seems ages, he stands motionless on the floor beside the bed, naked save for his dress socks, arms hanging straight down his sides, fingers twitching. The picture quality is too poor to see his eyes with any clarity, but they resemble gaping black holes on a blank white face that has been purged of any expression.

Slowly, and with great care, he begins to pick up his clothes which lie scattered across the floor.

He sits down on the end of the bed.

Pulls on his boxer shorts. His pants.

Then he's standing directly in front of the phone, pot belly taking up most of the frame.

Vincent leaves the room.

There is Paige, still motionless on the bed, and nothing else.

Finally, she sits up and looks around, bewildered.

Paige climbs down off the bed and walks over to the camera.

The picture swings up toward the ceiling.

The video ends.

"You okay, Paige?" he asked.

She gave a short, unconvincing nod, said, "A shame nobody from the church even bothered to call us back."

He powered off his sister's phone and looked at Sophie.

"What do you think?"

"I think I don't want to be inside this house anymore."

"Believe me now?"

"Believe what?"

"That something beyond our understanding is happening here."

"Yeah, and I want to leave, Grant. Does that strike you as a crazy request after what we just watched?"

"No, but—"

"But you don't trust me."

"I feel better with you here right now."

"And I just told you I don't want to be here. So are you going to continue to hold me against my will?"

Chapter 29

Paige blew out the candles and cleared the table while Grant moved Sophie into the living room. It was Friday night, and outside the street was busy with traffic heading downtown for the evening.

In an hour, Queen Anne would become a ghost town.

"It's getting cold in here," Sophie said, rubbing her shoulder with her free hand. "I can see my breath."

Grant exhaled and squinted into the air in front of him. "No you can't."

"It's still cold." She was right about that. The temperature was dropping fast. "Guess you haven't seen any of the weather reports."

"No, why?"

"First night below freezing."

"Awesome."

Through the window, the outline of a house appeared in soft, white Christmas lights. It was already mid-December, but the season had yet to see its first truly cold night. Terrible weather in return for a mild climate and a month of perfect summer—that was the Seattle contract. Wasn't for everyone, but Grant grooved on it. The cloudy skies jived with his ascetic inner-monk.

He surveyed the living room, eyes coming to rest on a mission-style rolling chair parked in front of a writing desk beside the fireplace. He pulled Sophie toward it, and then dragged the chair out and spun it around to face them.

Grant fished the key from his pocket and unlocked the bracelet around his wrist while keeping Sophie's from popping open.

He snapped it around the armrest of the rolling chair.

"Still think I'm a flight risk, huh?" she asked.

"I would be."

"And what if I looked you in the eyes and told you I wouldn't try to leave?"

"I couldn't live with myself putting you in a position to betray my trust."

She rolled her eyes and plopped down in the chair, rocked it back-and-forth.

Said, "What now?"

"I'm going to find something to burn. In the meantime..." he tugged the afghan he'd slept under the night before off the couch and flagged it open, "... try to stay warm."

He brought it down over Sophie.

"You're just going to leave me here with these wheels?"

"Knock yourself out. Take it for a spin."

Grant walked into the kitchen where Paige was still washing up.

"Can I help?" he asked.

"Water's cold," she said without turning around.

He walked up to the sink beside her, grabbed a plate.

"Thanks for dinner," he said as he submerged it in the frigid water.

Paige made no response.

"You were quiet," he said.

"Didn't want to incriminate myself anymore than *you* already have."

"Sophie's on our side."

"That why she's in handcuffs?"

Silence crept in between them.

Paige turned the water on again.

Grant could feel the tension in his sister like a living thing. Could see it in the furious concentric circles she made with the sponge across the surface of the plate.

"I heard you in the basement," she said at last.

Grant stopped scrubbing. Let the plate sink into the dishwater.

"Then you know I don't blame you for any of this."

"I know that if it comes down to my word against your partner's, I'm fucked."

"Hey, who's chained to a chair in your living room? You're my sister, all right? You get the benefit of the doubt."

"Why even bother? I'm a wreck, right? That's the word you used. A drug addict. A prostitute who fucked her own life from every position."

He said, "I was defending you, Paige," but it even sounded weak to him.

Her plate dropped into the water with a violent splash.

She put both hands on the edge of the sink.

"You've never defended me," she said.

"What are you talking about? I raised you."

"Not the same thing."

"That hurts more than you mean it to."

"Your crusade to fix me has always been about what I need, but never about what I need from you."

"I don't even know what that means, Paige."

"It means that I didn't need to be your project. I needed your support. I needed you to stand beside me."

"All I've ever wanted is to help you."

"I believe you think that. Just like any good doctor. But I'm not your patient. Want to know why I left the first time and why I kept leaving every time you found me?"

"Been asking myself that question for years."

"That's the problem. You don't have the answer, but you could never see that. I left because I got tired of watching you fumble with my problems like they were yours. Like you had the first clue about how to fix them. You're sicker than I am, Grant. All I wanted was a brother and all you wanted to be was a mechanic. We were both addicts."

"That's what family does. They try to help each other."

She turned to him.

"I got clean on my own, Grant. You show up and now we have a dead body upstairs and a police officer handcuffed in the living room. What exactly have you fixed?"

He grabbed the damp dishtowel from the counter and dried his hands.

"You make it sound like you've got your whole life sorted out. I just watched some guy use you, Paige. Maybe you're off drugs, but you're a helluva long way from clean."

The words were out before he could stop them. He was shocked by their venom, their precision. They had come from a place he didn't know existed, a place where there was no love for his sister. Just anger and disappointment.

Utter devastation arrived on her face.

She shook her head in bewilderment. "Fuck. You."

Chapter 30

"Everything okay?" Sophie called from her chair as Grant stormed through the foyer and into the living room.

"Fine," he said, selecting a short, squat candle that smelled like lavender from the flickering legion on the coffee table.

Grant went back into the foyer and made his way down the hall beside the stairs, stopping at the door to the basement. The tap continued to run in the kitchen. He listened for the clink of plates and glassware but there was no other sound. Imagined Paige standing frozen by the sink, the same mosaic of hurt across her face.

During that last intervention in Phoenix, when Paige was in the throes of a spectacular crash and burn, she had leaned over to Grant with tears in her eyes and whispered that she wished the car accident had left him a vegetable too. Then she'd kissed him on the cheek. That was Paige at her worst. Paige out of her mind. It hadn't made it any easier, but at least he'd known it wasn't his little sister saying those things.

So what's your excuse, pal? Around what can you hang the blame for your poison?

And yet still, it was there.

Unquenchable rage.

He stared across the kitchen at Paige's back.

Knew he shouldn't say it. Knew he should just let it go. Walk away. Punch a wall in private, but he couldn't stop himself. He never could. The acid wanted out, and it was coming.

He said, "Did you ever think for a minute that maybe I needed you? That maybe I needed a sister? Instead of a train wreck of a child who has not for one single day since I've known her had control of her own life? Has that thought ever crossed your mind? I guess I'm lucky I've never really needed you."

He opened the door and headed downstairs.

The candleflame faltered.

In the weak light, a few fragile stairs offered the way down before disappearing into darkness. Grant remembered how easily they had flexed under his weight before and placed his feet gingerly on the first step.

It bowed.

He could hear Paige crying in the kitchen. He hated it, but he wanted it.

He started down the stairs, staying at their edge and spending as little time on each step as possible without rushing the descent.

The darkness at the bottom was even thicker than he remembered. It seemed to congeal with the dank air like a viscous ether, cold and clammy on his skin.

Grant held the candle up and squinted, realizing that his eyes had already done all the adjusting they were going to do.

In the corner, the piano loomed, barely visible in the feeble illumination.

Something about its presence unsettled Grant, a part of him actually afraid that the darkness might blurt out some old rag time, the keys moving but no one at the helm. Sour notes where the hammers were missing or lame.

Grant put the brakes on that train of thought.

All those nights lying awake in bed, just a kid and no adult in the house, afraid to close his eyes—it was the same fear. He always thought he'd grow out of it. Still hoped he might. Hell, wasn't owning that fear part of the reason he'd been drawn to law enforcement? But adulthood had a way of making him feel like more of a child than when he'd actually been one.

Thirty-eight years old and still afraid of basements.

He took a moment to gather himself, and then made his way across the uneven stones to the window Sophie had smashed.

The fluorescent orb of a streetlight peered down at him through what remained of the glass.

Hunkered in the dark below it lay the buckled mass of the workbench. It was crudely made, a sheet of particleboard nailed to a pair of wooden sawhorses. The crew who'd done the remodel had probably left it behind. When Sophie had fallen through, she'd split the table top so that the two halves now met at a ninety degree angle. He didn't know if it would be enough, but it looked like perfect firewood.

Grant gave one of the halves a kick, hoping the wood might be soft enough to split with his foot.

The particleboard barely flexed.

A tremor of pain shot up his leg.

He turned and scanned the rest of the room for something he could use to break it up.

In the corner beneath the stairs, a cluster of long-handled tools rested against the wall.

He walked over and picked through the pile, finally selecting a sledgehammer which he hoisted and carried back to the workbench.

Grant set the candle on the floor beside him, and with his free hand, pulled both halves of the table away from the wall.

On the exposed brick in front of him, the unsteady light made his shadow tremble and curl onto the ceiling, the sledgehammer grotesquely elongated like a malformed limb.

The silhouette moved when he moved but it didn't feel like it belonged to him.

He threw an impulsive look back over his shoulder at the piano, but it was lost somewhere in darkness behind him.

He squared himself up in front of the bench.

Got a solid, two-handed grip—right hand under the head, left down toward the end of the handle—and raised the sledgehammer over his head.

The blow fell with such force that he didn't even feel it pass through the bench, splinters of wood exploding as the head crushed into the stone floor and sent a jarring shockwave up through his arms that rattled the fillings in his molars.

Eight more swings and the workbench had been reduced to a pile of kindling.

Panting, he leaned on the handle of the sledgehammer and examined the damage.

A good start, but not enough to burn through the night.

More importantly, not enough resistance to fill his need to destroy something.

Grant picked the candle up, threw the sledgehammer over his shoulder, and approached the corner where the piano sulked.

Up close, it was a gorgeous instrument. An upright Steinway of mahogany construction with brass gilding on the bass and treble ends. Must have been exquisite in its youth. Now, decades of exposure to the elements had stripped away most of the varnish and rusted its fixtures.

He propped the sledgehammer against one of its legs and ran his hand across the keyboard.

It was rough where the lacquered ivory had worn down to the wood beneath.

His index finger came to rest on middle C.

He pressed it.

The key sank with a gritty resistance, and for the first time in what Grant guessed might be decades, a single, decrepit note moaned from somewhere deep inside the old piano. It filled the basement, taking so long to dissipate that he began to feel unnerved at its continued presence.

It was still hanging in the air when the basement door opened and Paige's voice came to him from the top of the steps.

"What was that?"

"Nothing. Just getting some firewood."

Silence for a beat.

The door slammed.

Grant gave the piano one last look.

The note was gone, leaving only the hush of rain creeping in through the broken window.

He lifted the sledgehammer, heaved it above his head, and sent it crashing through the wooden lid, down into the guts where it severed the remaining strings in a horrible twanging cacophony.

The resistance was glorious.

He drank it in.

Ripped the head out, swung again.

And again.

And again.

And again.

Chapter 31

It took him three trips to carry up all the fruits of his rage.

As he sat on the hearth arranging balls of newsprint and kindling under the grate, Sophie said, "You're drenched with sweat. Everything okay?"

"Not so much."

"Paige has been crying in the kitchen."

"We had words."

"Yeah, I heard some of them."

He laid two legs of the piano bench across the grate and grabbed the box of matches.

Struck a light, held it to the paper.

As the flame spread, it suddenly hit him—exhaustion.

Total, mind-melting exhaustion.

The kindling ignited.

"I'm gonna be turning in soon," he said. "You need to use the bathroom or anything?"

"You just destroyed her in there. You know that, right?"

He looked at Sophie.

Dishes clanged in the kitchen sink.

"I know she's hurt you," Sophie said. "I know she's disappointed you. I know she's been a pain in your ass since the two of you were on your own. I get all of that. But for whatever reason, you got one sister in your life, and there won't be anymore. I got none. I envy you."

"Sophie—"

"I understand that I don't understand what it's like."

"The things she does to herself," he said. "That she lets these men do to her for money."

"I know."

"I remember when she was six years old. When she had nothing in the world but me."

"I know."

"And now this?"

"Grant—"

"I love her so much."

He wiped his eyes, piled more wood onto the fire.

Grant took Sophie to the bathroom and then set her up in a leather recliner. He cuffed her right ankle to the metal framework under the footrest and buried her under a mass of blankets.

Her phone vibrated in his pocket.

He tugged it out, swiped the screen.

Art had sent another text, this one carrying an attachment.

It was a photo of the interior of a diner.

Four men seated at a booth.

"What is it?" Sophie asked.

He showed her the pic and pointed to the frumpy-looking man seated next to Jude Grazer.

"Steve Vincent," she said.

"Yep. The gang's all there."

A local number appeared on the screen.

"Recognize it?" Grant asked.

"That's Frances."

He answered with, "That was fast."

"I aim to please."

"You got something?"

"Mr. Flowers has a couple of DUIs."

"That's it?"

"That's it. No ViCAP hits. No NCIC. But … I did run everyone through the Social Security Death Index on our Ancestry.com account."

"Good thinking, and?"

"Williams, Janice D., died March 2, 2007. She was forty-one. I don't know if that's helpful. I don't have any other information."

"The other tenants are still warm and breathing?"

"Yes."

"This is super helpful, Frances. Thank you."

"I've got another call coming in—"

"Take it. I owe you big time."

Grant ended the call.

Sophie looked up at him, eyebrows raised.

"One second," he said.

He hurried out of the living room, through the foyer, and into the dining room, where he grabbed Stu's manila folder off the table.

Through the open doorway, he caught a glimpse of Paige still at the kitchen sink.

He jogged back to Sophie and sat down in proximity to the only decent light in the house—the roaring fire—and opened the folder.

"Talk to me, Grant. What are you suddenly cranked up about?"

"No meaningful hits on any database, but Frances ran all the names to see if anyone had died. One did, five years ago."

"Do you know how old they were at time of death?"

"Only forty-one."

He scrolled the list.

Four names down from the top, he found Janice Williams.

"Hmm," he said.

"What?"

"Ms. Williams died while she was still living here."

"So? People die. It happens."

"You aren't a little bit curious for more details?"

"Is there contact info on the spreadsheet?"

"Just a phone number. Must be next-of-kin."

"Call 'em up."

Grant dialed. "Five-oh-nine area code," he said. "Recognize it?"

"Spokane."

It rang five times, and then went to the voice mail of a gruff, tired-sounding man with a blue-collar twang. Grant pictured a mechanic.

You reached Robert. I can't get to the phone right at this moment. Leave your name and number and I will call you back.

After the beep, Grant left his name and Sophie's cell.

"You warm yet?" he asked her.

"Getting there. What now?"

"We sleep. Then first thing tomorrow, we'll call every resident on that list. We'll find out what happened to Ms. Williams, have Stu dig up her death certificate, whatever it takes."

"And Rachel."

"What?"

"We call Don's wife. No matter what."

"Yes. Absolutely."

Her skin was beautiful in the firelight, and in that moment, if Sophie had asked him to let her go, he probably would have done it.

Grant crawled onto the sofa and under a blanket.

He took out Sophie's phone—the battery charge had dropped to thirty percent—and powered it off.

Then he rolled onto his side, faced the fire.

The movement of the flames was mesmerizing.

He shut his eyes for a minute, and the next time he opened them, the fire was low and Paige was lying on the mattress below him, staring up at the ceiling.

"What if she's right, Grant?" she said.

"Who?"

"Sophie."

"About?"

"About me."

He wasn't following. He'd been sleeping too hard.

"What are you talking about, Paige?"

"About all of this having to do with me. What if it's not the house that's haunted?"

"I don't believe that."

"Because you don't want to?"

"Look, I don't know what this thing is, but I do know you, Paige."

"Do you really?"

Chapter 32

It is the strangest sensation, the closest thing to a lucid dream she's ever experienced.

She is aware of herself asleep on the recliner.

She feels the leather cushions beneath her but also the sensation of existing outside of herself. Like being in the audience of a play while she's also onstage.

There is another, more ominous sensation.

Someone standing over her.

She can feel their presence.

Hovering.

Watching.

She wants to turn her head but won't, thinking that whatever is standing next to the chair is waiting for her to look, and that as soon as she does, it will do the thing it wants to do so badly.

This must be limbo, she thinks.

This is what forever is going to be like for me.

But that idea is somehow worse, and she's already turning her head.

Sophie looks up and opens her eyes.

The fire is so low that the room stands in virtual darkness.

Rain drums against the windows.

It stands beside the chair, staring down into her face.

Not Paige. Not Grant.

Just a pure black shadow shorter than either of them, with long, skinny arms that nearly touch the floor.

She tries to speak, but her mouth won't open.

Tries to turn away, but she has lost the mobility of her lucid dream, now locked in a stare with the shadow.

That she cannot see a single detail of its face is somehow worse.

Her mind runs in terrible directions.

The next time she blinks, the shadow has changed.

Replaced by a profile she knows.

The dying fire even lends this face a glimmer of color.

Paige Moreton says, "Why won't you talk to me?"

Her eyes are shining, and she is smiling.

Chapter 33

Grant woke from a troubled sleep to the sound of someone whispering his name.

It was still night.

The fire had burned itself down to a bed of embers, and despite the blankets that covered him, he was shivering violently.

"Grant."

It was Sophie.

He pulled the covers tighter around his neck.

"What's up?" he whispered.

"Come here."

"Something wrong?"

"Just come here."

Grant kicked back the covers and swung his legs off the sofa.

The hardwood floor was ice under his feet.

He moved quietly over to Sophie's chair which he'd positioned at the foot of Paige's mattress.

Knelt down beside her.

"I had a dream," she said.

"A nightmare?"

"Yeah."

"What happened?"

"I was sleeping in this chair, and there was this presence beside me. I could feel it so clearly. It's like I was half-awake. I tried not to look, because I knew that's what it wanted me to do, but I finally gave in. It was just a shadow and I couldn't see its face. Then suddenly Paige was standing there instead."

"Paige was in your dream?"

"And she was smiling. Something about it was off, though."

Grant glanced back at his sister sleeping peacefully in the ember light.

Sophie said, "She asked why I wasn't talking to her. Then I woke up. What do you think?"

"Honestly? Sounds about right considering the day we've had. My dreams sucked too."

"It was more than a nightmare, Grant. I know what a dream feels like."

"What was it then?"

"Communication."

"Oh. You think our friend upstairs wants a word?"

"You're mocking me."

"I promise you I'm not, but would we be having this conversation if it had told you to come up and crawl under the bed?"

"Of course not."

"That's what it wants."

"How do you know?"

"Because that's what I see in *my* dreams. It wants me in that room. Under the bed."

"So it's talking to you too."

"I don't know. Maybe. But I'm not going in there to find out."

"We don't have to. What if we just stay in the hall? Try to talk to it through the door."

"You really think that's a good idea?"

"What's the alternative? Do nothing while our little world in here continues to fall apart?"

"We're not doing nothing, Sophie. Tomorrow, we're gonna track down Janice Williams and find out what happened to her. Maybe that blows everything open for us."

"And maybe it doesn't. The clock is ticking. It's a matter of time before you and I are officially MIA. And what about Don? You know Rachel has already reported him missing."

"Look, I'm aware of the stakes, okay? But I'm not ready to start chasing dreams. I say we stick to whatever shreds of reality we still have left. That's where we'll find our answers."

"You don't know the first thing about what's going on here so don't pretend you can tell the difference between what's real and what's not."

"Fine," he said. "What if it is trying to talk to us, and all it really wants to say is 'I'm gonna torture and kill you assholes.' Then what?"

"Then we confirm what we already know. And I'd rather know—good or bad—than remain in this state of total darkness we're in right now."

She had a point.

It wasn't the first time.

Their options were exhausted, and the idea of waking up in this house, of spending another day in this prison, was more than he could face. A time would come when it would be too much. When it would break him. He could feel that moment fast-approaching.

"All right," he said. "I'll wake Paige."

"No." Sophie grabbed his arm.

"Why not?"

"Just let her sleep."

"This is a big decision. She deserves to be involved."

"Let's just you and I go up."

"Is it because of your dream? Because you think she's playing some part in this?"

"I don't know. Just a gut feeling that it should only be you and me."

Grant unlocked the bracelet around Sophie's ankle and gave her a hand up out of the chair.

"No cuffs?" she said.

"No cuffs."

She lit a pair of candles while he went to the sofa and pulled the Glock out from between the cushions.

He waited until they'd reached the foyer before digging the magazine out of his pocket, driving it home, and jacking a round into the chamber.

Sophie went up first, the steps creaking under her bare feet.

It was ungodly cold and the chill intensified the higher they climbed.

By the time they reached the second floor, it was freezing, their exhalations pluming white in the candlelight.

They rounded the corner and stopped.

The door to Paige's room stood shut at the far end of the corridor.

Grant could hear the rain drumming on the roof.

The elevated *boom-boom-boom* of his heart.

Nothing else.

He was wide awake now, operating on sensory overdrive—everything heightened but his diminished sense of sight.

Sophie headed down the hall and he followed.

They passed the small table at the midpoint and continued on until they stood shoulder-to-shoulder, the door looming three feet ahead.

Grant kept swallowing, trying to make his ears pop, but they wouldn't.

Sophie whispered, "Go ahead."

"Why are you whispering?"

"I don't know. What are you waiting for?"

"This is weird."

"Aren't you used to weird by now?"

"Should I knock?"

She shot him a look. "Take it seriously."

Grant cleared his throat and took a step forward.

"Is anyone in there?" he said.

They barely breathed.

Thirty seconds passed in silence.

"Guess we have our answer," Grant said, turning to leave.

"Try it louder."

"I feel like I'm just talking to a door."

"Don't you ever pray?"

"Not anymore."

"Pretend there's something on the other side that can hear you. Show it respect."

"This is ridiculous."

"Get closer."

He turned to her. "You want to do this?"

Grant stepped up to the door again, so close he could feel the icy draft issuing from the crack at the bottom. He braced himself on either side of the frame.

"This is Grant Moreton. I'm Paige's brother. She's the woman who lives here."

He looked back at Sophie.

She nodded him on.

"Can you tell me what it is you want?"

He put his ear to the door.

Silence again.

No sound on the second floor but the rain striking the roof.

"This is Ouija board shit," he said.

"Keep going."

"What do you want?" Grant said, louder.

No answer.

"What. Do. You. Want."

Grant felt Sophie's hand touch his shoulder. He was beginning to churn with the first bubblings of rage, a mad impulse creeping in to kick the door in, Glock drawn. Shoot the room to pieces.

"Why won't you let us leave?"

Nothing.

Yelling now—*"Why are you here?"*

Sophie grabbed his arm but he ripped free and beat his fist against the door.

She said, "Maybe you're asking the wrong questions."

"Are you asleep? Are we disturbing you? 'Cause you're sure as hell disturbing us." He punched the door. "Wake up and talk to me."

He turned away and started back down the hallway.

When he reached the table, he glanced over his shoulder and stopped.

Sophie still stood facing the door which was bathed in the light of her candles.

"Hey," Grant said. "You're my light source. Come on. We're done here."

She didn't move.

"Sophie?"

She looked at him, and then back at the door.

When she shouted, it startled him so much he flinched.

"What are you?"

Her voice raged through the second-floor corridors, and its echo had not quite faded into silence when every light in the hallway blazed on with a retina-burning intensity.

The building rumbled as the central heating kicked.

A ceiling fan above Grant's head began to whir.

The phone in his pocket vibrated to life.

Sophie faced him, shielding her eyes and squinting against the sudden onslaught of light.

She had just opened her mouth to speak when a noise from below rushed up the staircase and drove a spear of terror through Grant's heart.

A scream.

Paige.

The Glock was in his hand and he was running before he'd even thought to react, socks sliding across the carpet as he turned the corner, his shoulder crashing into the wall.

He righted himself and bolted for the stairs.

Took them two at a time, his footfalls pounding down the steps.

Five from the bottom, he jumped.

His sock-feet hit the hardwood floor of the foyer and he skidded to a stop under the archway that opened into the living room.

Paige stood beside the recliner holding Sophie's purse.

She looked bleary-eyed and horror-stricken.

Grant said, "What happened?"

Sophie came tearing off the stairs into the foyer.

She stopped beside Grant, said, "What are you doing with my purse, Paige?"

"What is *this*, Sophie?"

Paige shook a scrap of paper in her right hand.

Grant walked over. "What is it?"

She handed him a badly-wrinkled receipt from The Whisky, brittle from water damage.

Paige said, "Other side."

Grant flipped it.

"It was in her purse."

Grant stared at Sophie.

"Why do you have this?"

"That's the receipt I found in Seymour's hand. I told you about it on the phone, remember?"

"Benjamin Seymour was holding this?"

"Yes, at the Japanese garden in the arboretum. What am I missing? Why is your sister going through my purse?"

"This is our father."

"What does this mean, Grant?" Paige asked.

Grant stared at the portrait. "I don't know."

Sophie said, "I wasn't trying to keep it from you. I had no idea."

The cell in Grant's pocket vibrated.

He jammed the Glock into the back of his waistband, grabbed the phone, swiped the screen.

A series of texts from Art Dobbs had just uploaded.

10:06 p.m.
diner closing, they're leaving

10:13 p.m.
they went across street to bar

12:01 a.m.
still here, you so owe me

2:02 a.m.
last call, they're leaving

Grant glanced at the current time—2:37 a.m.

Paige said, "Sophie, I can't explain why I even opened your purse. When the power came on, I woke up and I was just standing here. The receipt was already in my hand. I wasn't snooping, I swear. What were you guys doing upstairs?"

Grant said, "I heard something. We went up to check."

"What was it?"

"I don't know. The power came on, you screamed, I ran back down."

Sophie's phone buzzed again.

Grant glanced down—Dobbs calling.

"Here." He tossed Sophie her phone.

"He's gonna be pissed," she said. "Probably thinks I just bailed on him."

"Blame me."

Sophie answered on speakerphone: "Hey, superstar, what's up?"

"Oh, not too much. Just doing your job at two thirty-seven in the morning when I should be home in bed with my wife. Hope I didn't interrupt *your* beauty sleep."

"I'm so sorry," she said. "I'm at Grant's. He's having a real hard time. Major bender."

The sarcasm vanished. "Sorry to hear that. I don't mean to be an asshole. I'm just exhausted."

"What's the news?"

"You see my texts?"

"No."

"Our boys are on the move. They left a bar in North Bend about thirty minutes ago after sitting at a table for four hours, drinking nothing but water and barely even speaking to each other. Grazer and the new guy arrived separately, but they all left together in a black GMC Savana. New model. In all my free time, I ran the plates. Car was rented yesterday morning in Bellevue on Talbert's Visa."

"Where are you right now?" Sophie asked.

"They just turned north onto the four-oh-five."

Grant looked at Paige.

He could see it in her eyes. She'd made the connection too.

"Thanks, Art. Keep me posted."

When Sophie had ended the call, Grant said, "I know where they're going."

"Where?" Sophie asked.

"Kirkland."

"What's in Kirkland?"

Grant held up the receipt.

"Our father," Paige said.

Chapter 34

For ten seconds, no one spoke.

Sophie finally broke the silence, "Are you sure?"

"A hundred percent? No. But his hospital is in Kirkland."

"Why would they be going to see your father?"

"I couldn't begin to answer that." Grant pulled out Sophie's Glock, crossed the room, gave it to her. "He's at Evergreen Psychiatric Hospital. His name is James Moreton. Call Art on your way, tell him what's going on. Please stop whatever is about to happen, since there's not a damn thing I can do, stuck in this house."

Sophie went to the chair and pulled on her boots and jacket, took her purse back from Paige.

"Let me have your phone," Grant said, the helplessness and frustration beginning to ferment into rage.

She handed it over, and he typed in a number.

"What are you doing?" she asked.

"Programming my sister's number so you can reach us."

At the front door, Grant unlocked the dead bolts and the chain.

It couldn't have been more than a few degrees above freezing, their breath steaming as they stepped out onto the porch.

At the bottom of the steps, Grant felt something like a shiv slide in at the base of his skull.

Sophie said, "The pain's back?"

"I'm not going to be able to leave. How are you feeling?"

"Fine."

"Then go while you can."

She embraced him.

"I'll call you. Be careful, Grant."

"You too."

She rushed off into the rain and turned left when she hit the sidewalk. Grant watched her cross the empty street and climb into her TrailBlazer.

The engine growled to life, the tires screeched against the wet pavement, and Sophie roared off down the street.

He forced himself to take another step.

Pain ignited in the pit of his stomach and flashed through the rest of his body with the velocity of a shaped charge.

He doubled over.

Only when he staggered back did the agony wane.

In its place, that molten rage poured in.

By the time he reached the top of the steps, Grant had gone supernova.

He moved through the door, back into the house.

Paige stood in the foyer, arms crossed as if they were the only thing holding her together.

She was crying, trembling.

She said, "Now what?"

He went past her into the kitchen, liberated a knife from the cutlery block.

Rushed back down the hallway.

Up the stairs.

Paige calling after him.

He didn't answer.

As he reached the top, he heard her footsteps climbing toward him.

He rounded the corner.

Turned down the hallway.

Wasn't that he didn't care or feel the fear. But as had happened a handful of times in his life, everything—absolutely everything—had been overridden by a pure and blinding need to break something. To destroy. There was something inside of him that had formed when his mother died and grown when his father was incapacitated, and had just kept festering and rotting through his orphaned childhood, while he struggled to provide for and raise Paige, into adolescence as he watched his sister derail, into adulthood when their estrangement solidified. It was the rage of a life frustrated, lonely, unfair, and devoid of anything approaching a single stroke of luck or good fortune.

It was why he got blackout drunk.

Why he went to bars in the sticks to get in fights.

Why he fucked prostitutes.

And why he was about to kick in the goddamn door to Paige's room and once inside, tear whatever he found apart with his bare hands.

"Grant!"

He stopped halfway down the corridor, looked back at his sister.

She said, "Don't do this."

"Why? Because something bad might happen to me? That'd be a real change of pace, wouldn't it?"

"Please. Come downstairs. We'll talk this through. We'll figure out our next step. I need you."

Grant smiled. He felt electrified. Amped on methamphetamines. Like he could punch through brick.

He said, "I'm done talking."

Then he turned and ran at Paige's door, the pressure mounting in his head, a small voice asking if he was sure he wanted to do this but it was too late.

Inside of three feet, he raised his right leg and snapped his heel into the center of the door.

It exploded back.

Paige screaming his name.

His foot throbbing.

He crossed the threshold, and the moment he was standing fully inside, the door slammed shut behind him.

Chapter 35

The pressure in his head was enormous. Like sitting at the bottom of the ocean.

He couldn't hear Paige anymore.

Couldn't hear the rain on the roof.

Not even the mad thumping of his heart.

There was a single source of illumination—a salt lamp resting atop a chest of drawers at the foot of Paige's bed. The fractured crystal put out a soft orange glow that failed to reach the corners of the room.

Grant's vision doubled.

The lamp split into two orbs of light.

He blinked and they came back together.

The pressure swelled inside his eyes, his lungs struggling with each breath to inflate.

A stabbing pain thrummed through his inner ear in time with his pulse.

Fighting the disorientation, he tried to tune back into the rage that had brought him here.

He grabbed the salt lamp and tightened his grip on the knife.

A dust ruffle skirted the bed, an inch of blackness between the hem and the floor.

Grant stumbled toward it and dropped to his hands and knees, the fog in his head thickening fast, thoughts and intentions flattening under the pressure.

He put the side of his head on the floor and reached for the dust ruffle.

Some remote part of his brain screaming at him to stand up, turn around, get out, but its voice was growing quieter every second.

Under the bed.

He was staring under the bed.

He'd walked into his sister's house thirty hours ago, and since then he'd been fighting this moment. Why had he resisted?

The light in his hand spilled into the darkness.

Dusty hardwood floor.

A pile of blankets.

Grant pushed the light forward, dragging himself behind it.

As his head passed beneath the bed frame, he registered a peculiar smell.

Vinegar and electrical burn.

The blankets shifted.

Grant reached out, took hold, pulled them aside.

The light eked onto two sacs of spider eggs—rust colored clusters that resembled the overripe drupelets of blackberries.

As Grant stared at them, a translucent membrane slid over one, and then the other, and retracted simultaneously.

The pressure in his head vanished. He dropped the knife.

Not spider eggs. Eyes. He was staring into a pair of eyes.

From behind the blankets, a long, slender arm shot out, and fingers encircled his neck.

It is dark and he is not alone.
There is nothing before, nothing after.
It is all and only now.
The floor beneath him rushes away. His stomach lifts. He's gripped with the sensation of falling at an inconceivable speed, hurtling through darkness

at what has been pulling him toward this room since he first set foot in the house.

He crashes into a terrible intellect.

For the first time in his life, he is aware—truly aware—of his mind. Its weakness and vulnerability. His skull is a pitiful firewall. The invasion effortless. Everything he loves and hates and fears is unhoused, his private circuitry torn out and laid bare.

Before Grant can even wonder what it wants, it is unrolling his mind like a parchment.

He feels the synaptic structure of his brain changing, being rebuilt, reprogrammed.

The tingle of neuron fire.

Thoughts he's never had materialize as if they've always been.

A sequence of directions take shape.

Right turns and left turns.

Street names.

All at once, his mind cauterizes shut, and he is left with the absolute knowledge of what he must do next.

The eyes blink again.

The floor returns.

He is no longer under the bed but standing beside it and cradling something in a tangle of blankets.

Chapter 36

At three o'clock in the morning, Mercer was empty enough for Sophie to burn through red lights at full speed.

She hit the I-5 and screamed north to 520.

Dialed Art halfway across Lake Washington and stuck him on speaker so she could keep two hands on the wheel while she did ninety-five over wet concrete, the windshield wipers frantically whipping across the glass.

Art answered with, "Hey, Sophie."

"Where are you?"

"Still on the four-oh-five, couple miles south of Kirkland."

"They may be going to the Evergreen Psychiatric Hospital."

"How do you know that?"

"Long story, but I'm on my way, about five minutes behind you."

"Why are they going to this hospital?"

"No idea, but Grant's father lives there. Seymour had drawn a weird picture of him on a receipt. Didn't connect the dots until a few minutes ago."

"And you think they're going after him?"

"Possibly. I'm calling the hospital right now and putting them on notice so they can scramble security."

"I'll call for backup."

Sophie depressed the brake pedal as she veered onto an exit ramp, nearly lost control of the TrailBlazer at the end as she whipped it around, tires skidding on the wet road, the SUV tipping up on two wheels for a terrifying instant.

She managed to right the car and stomp the gas, now accelerating north up Lake Washington Boulevard.

The city just a foggy glow across the water.

"Art," she said. "I have no idea what these men are all about."

"You and me both."

"So do me a favor, huh?"

"What's that?"

"Don't get yourself shot."

Chapter 37

Grant opened the door and walked out into the corridor.
    Paige stood several feet away, tears streaming down her face.
    "I tried to open it, but it wouldn't budge. I thought something had—"
    "I'm okay."
    "You're sure?"
    "Yeah."
    She looked down at the blanket in Grant's arms.
    "Is that what I think it is?"
    He nodded.
    She brought her hand to her mouth.
    When she reached toward the blanket, Grant took a step back.
    "I just want to see," she said.
    She took hold of the end of the blanket.
    Raised it.
    "Oh my God."

Chapter 38

The Evergreen Psychiatric Hospital on the outskirts of Kirkland was a four-story brick monstrosity that stretched across twenty acres of conifer-studded lawns.

Sophie's TrailBlazer raced up the narrow drive.

The buildings appeared in the distance.

Through the rain-streaked windshield, she could see a smattering of glowing windows, but most of the facade stood dark.

She whipped into the circle drive at the front entrance, killed the engine.

3:13 a.m.

She pulled her Glock, checked the load.

Out into the cold and pouring rain.

She jogged over to Art's Dodge Diplomat—a pimped-out relic from the old days. The driver's side door was open, the interior dome light on, but the car empty.

Just prior to the roundabout, the driveway had branched into a vast parking lot, and on the far side, under the dripping branches of a Douglas-fir, she spotted the black van.

She ran toward it. The rain had escalated from a drizzle to a downpour since she'd left the house, gusting sideways across the desolate parking lot, the light poles swaying.

She moved along the edge where the eastern perimeter of Douglas-firs offered cover from the streetlights.

Twenty feet away, she came out of the trees.

The van wasn't running.

The front seats were empty, but from the side, with its deeply-tinted windows, she couldn't see anything in the back.

She approached it head on, Glock aimed through the windshield.

No lights on inside.

No movement.

She tried the driver side door, but it was locked.

By the time Sophie had returned to the main entrance, she was soaked. She climbed the stone steps and pushed through the front doors and, finally, out of the rain.

In the vestibule, she stopped, jacket dripping on the linoleum, and took out her phone.

Tried Art for the third time in the last five minutes.

Same result.

It rang four times and dumped her into voice mail.

Sophie pushed through the inner doors into a large reception area bathed in the punishing glow of high-wattage fluorescent lights. Moved quickly toward the front desk where a nurse in blue scrubs was scribbling on a patient chart.

The smell of the place was insidious—notes of Clorox, Lysol, stewed green vegetables, desperation.

Sophie had her shield out by the time the woman looked up.

Mid-thirties, attractive despite the total absence of makeup, and surprisingly clear-eyed for the late hour.

"Detective Benington, Seattle PD. Did another detective come through here? Fifties, little overweight, balding—"

The nurse was already shaking her head.

"Nobody but you has walked through those front doors since I came on shift at midnight."

"His car's out front."

"Well, he didn't come this way."

"You didn't hear him pull up?"

"Kind of been busy." She held up a folder. "Thirty-five patient charts to complete before eight a.m."

"I spoke to your head of security about five minutes ago, told him there was a possible threat to one of your patients. Jim Moreton."

"I don't know anything about that. I'm sorry, but without a signed release I can't discuss any patients or even confirm that the person you just mentioned is actually a patient here."

Sophie leaned in. "Is there another entrance to this facility?"

"On the north side, but it's only open and staffed during visiting hours."

"I need you to take me to Jim Moreton right now."

"Ma'am, HIPAA is pretty clear on the protection of patient privacy."

"How about the protection of their physical safety?"

"Ma'am, I—"

"Do you understand what I'm telling you? Men may have come here to kill Mr. Moreton."

The woman stonewalled.

"Tell me you understand what I just said," Sophie pushed.

"I understand."

"And you're refusing to take me to him so I can check on his welfare? You believe the intent of HIPAA is to prevent a law enforcement officer from checking on the welfare of a psychiatric patient who may be in grave and immediate danger?"

Two gunshots erupted, muffled and distant.

The nurse's eyes grew big.

Sophie pulled her Glock. "Where is he?"

"Acute unit."

Another gunshot, different caliber.

"Tell me how to get there."

The nurse rose from behind the desk and came around to Sophie.

"I'll have to take you. It's like a maze, and doors don't open without an ID badge."

Sophie followed her out of reception and down a long corridor.

"Are more police coming?" the nurse asked.

"Yes, on their way. What's your name?"

"Angela."

"I'm Sophie."

"I'm sorry I didn't—"

"Forget it."

They picked up the pace, now moving through a series of intersecting short corridors that Sophie would have never been able to navigate on her own.

Straight ahead, the way was blocked by a pair of double doors, each with a square of glass inset at eye level.

Angela unclipped her ID from her scrubs and reached for the card-swipe.

"Hold that thought," Sophie said, waving her off.

She leaned into the glass window and stared through. The hallway on the other side ran perpendicular to this corridor, and her field of vision only extended for several feet each way beyond the doors.

Sophie strained to listen—nothing but Angela's elevated respirations and the ever-present hum of the lights overhead.

"All right," Sophie said. "Go ahead and swipe it, but I want you to hang back until I give the all clear."

The internal locking mechanism buzzed.

Deadbolts retracted.

Sophie pulled open one of the doors, stepped over the threshold.

She poked her head out into the corridor and glanced both ways.

Nothing but miles of empty linoleum.

Sophie whispered over her shoulder, "All right, come on."

Angela led her down a corridor that shot between two larger buildings.

The windows on either side were barred, rainwater streaming down the glass.

"What's going on exactly?" the nurse asked.

"I'm not a hundred percent sure. Have you worked with Mr. Moreton?"

"Yes."

"Is he locked in his room each night?"

"And medicated. He's a threat to himself and others."

The corridor banked into a building, and they arrived at another pair of doors, these windowless and steel-reinforced.

"What's on the other side?" Sophie asked.

"Acute."

Sophie put her ear against the door. Over the clamor of her own heart, she thought she heard voices, though she couldn't be sure.

"Angela, give me your ID." The nurse handed it over without hesitation. "Now I want you to run back down the corridor as far as you can. Find a room without windows and lock yourself inside. Go now."

The nurse turned and hurried off down the hall, the soles of her Keds sliding across the linoleum as she turned a hard corner and disappeared.

Sophie waited until the echo of her retreating footsteps had almost faded away. Then she turned the card over, lined up the magnetic strip, swiped it through.

The sudden buzz of the locks retracting unleashed a new belt of adrenaline.

She shoved the card into the inner pocket of her jacket, tugged open one of the doors, and got a solid two-handed grip on her Glock as a quiet voice in the back of her mind whispered, *You've never even drawn your weapon in the field, much less shot it. 'Lil bit different than the range.*

Straight ahead, a nurses' station.

Two corridors branched off behind it on either side.

She heard that noise again—what she'd thought were voices from the other side of the doors.

Crying.

Someone whispering, *Shut up.*

The stifled, high-pitched hyperventilation of a person in hysterics fighting to hold it back.

It was all coming from behind the nurses' station.

Sophie sited it down the barrel of her G22 and announced herself, "Seattle PD. Who's behind the desk?"

A deep, male voice said, "It's three of us. We work in this unit."

"I need you to stand up for me. One at a time, very slowly. Keeping your hands interlocked behind your head."

"We can't."

"Why?"

"They tied us up."

"Who did?"

"Four men."

"Are they still on this wing?"

"I don't know."

"What did they want?"

"They asked where Jim Moreton was. They took my ID card and my key ring."

Sophie moved forward toward the nurses' station.

When she reached it, she rose up on the balls of her feet and peeked over the edge of the desk. Two orderlies and a nurse lay on their stomachs on the floor, wrists and ankles bound with Zip Ties.

The smell of gunpowder was strong. It competed with the sweet bite of urine. The nurse was lying in a pool of it, her scrubs around her crotch darkened.

"Anyone injured?"

Headshakes.

"I heard gunshots. Were they armed?"

The nurse's mascara had run all to hell, her black-rimmed eyes swollen with fear.

She nodded. "Yes, two of them."

"Where did they go?"

"Jim Moreton's room."

Sophie kept scoping each corridor and glancing back at the double doors she'd come through moments ago. Tactically, this was a dangerous spot—centrally located and vulnerable to multiple points of attack.

She said, "Did another police officer come through here?"

"I think so."

She yelled, "Art!"

There was no response.

The nurse continued, "I didn't see him—we were already tied up—but I heard him yell 'police' and then the shooting started."

"What room is Jim Moreton in?"

"Seven-sixteen. Down the hall to the right."

Sophie started toward the corridor.

"You're just leaving us here?" the nurse cried.

"Backup's on the way. Stay quiet."

"Please!" she begged. "Don't leave us!"

"Shut up!"

A door slammed somewhere on the wing.

Sophie exploded down the corridor, the heels of her boots pummeling the tile.

Room 701 blurred past.

Full sprint now.

702.

Heart thudding through the slats of her ribcage.

706.

707.

Her elbow clipped a rolling IV stand that toppled hard and went skating across the floor.

713.

714.

715.

She slowed to a stop a few feet away from Moreton's room. The door was cracked, but no light escaped.

Her lungs burned.

Somewhere on the wing, a patient banged against the inside of their door and warbled incoherently.

Sophie leaned back on the wooden handrail that ran the length of the hallway and inched forward. The smell of gunpowder was strongest here, and under the fluorescent glare, something glinted on the floor—a .40 cal shell casing.

One of Art's.

Deep breaths.

716.

A small pane of reinforced glass looked into the room.

She peered through the bottom corner of the window.

A little light bled through a curtain on the far side of the room, but it only brightened several tiles on the floor. Everything else lay in shadow.

She eased the door open.

It swung on its hinges without a sound.

Light from the hallway spilled across the floor.

Reaching in, she palmed the wall, running her hand along the smooth concrete until it grazed a light switch.

She hesitated.

Glanced up and down the corridor.

Nothing moved.

That nurse was crying again and the patient beating his door even harder, but she relegated these superfluous distractions to background noise.

She hit the switch—two fluorescent panels flickering to life—and then dug her shoulder into the door and charged.

The door crashed hard into the rubber stop on the wall and bounced back, but she was already past and swinging into the bleak little room.

There was a single bed lined with metal railing and occupied by Jim Moreton.

The man lay on his side under a white blanket, his back to her.

She cleared the far side of the bed and then opened a door beside a dresser, groping for the light switch.

A small bathroom appeared.

She stepped in, swept back the shower curtain.

Cleared the toilet alcove.

She was breathing so hard her vision had begun to populate with throbbing motes of blackness.

She went to the closet, opened the sliding doors.

Ten pairs of identical khaki slacks. Ten long-sleeved button-down shirts—all variations of blue. Three pairs of Velcro shoes.

Otherwise, empty.

She turned her attention to the bed. The wrist she could see wore a padded restraint that was attached to the railing by a leather loop.

"Mr. Moreton?"

As she moved toward the bed, the face on Seymour's receipt flashed through her mind.

Sunken cheeks. Frown lines like canyons in his forehead. Wild, stringy hair.

The hairline on the back of this man's head was cropped, and it ran back to a patchy area at the top of his scalp where it had begun to thin.

She knew that bald spot.

Sat behind it every day at the precinct.

Sophie rolled Art Dobbs onto his back.

The left side of his face resembled an eggplant, swollen and shiny. His eye had disappeared into it and the other was turned up into its socket like a cue ball.

"Art."

She shook him.

Then ripped back the covers.

No blood.

"Art, can you hear me?"

A gurgling noise issued from his nose as air struggled through the grotesque new angle of his nasal cavity.

He was out cold, but at least he was breathing, and he wasn't shot.

She dialed 911, held her phone between her shoulder and ear as she headed out of the room.

"Nine-one-one, where is your emergency?"

"Evergreen Psychiatric Hospital in Kirkland. This is Detective Benington with the Seattle PD." Sophie edged out into the corridor. "Shots fired, officer down. Art Dobbs is in room seven-sixteen in the acute unit." Started moving at a jog. "Four suspects. Armed. Driving a black GMC Savana. They may have kidnapped Jim Moreton, a patient here." She was approaching an intersection, the floor up ahead smeared with what appeared to be blood.

"What are his injuries?"

"I have to go now—"

"Ma'am, please—"

Sophie ended the call, slid the phone back into her jacket.

The blood smear wasn't isolated. Footprints—the tread of a dress shoe—continued on.

She swung around the corner and sited down the corridor.

The prints trailed off after a few steps, but the blood trail didn't.

There was a man sitting against the wall under an exit sign that burned red at the far end—didn't look like Moreton, but she couldn't be sure from this distance.

Sophie called out, "Seattle Police! Get on your stomach and spread out your hands!"

The man was fifty feet away.

He turned his head and stared at her but failed to move.

"Did you not hear me, sir? Do you want to get shot?"

He said, "I'm already shot."

As Sophie moved forward, she saw that he wasn't lying. The man held his right leg with both hands and he sat in a small, dark pool that reflected the fluorescents redly.

Good for you, Art.

At thirty feet, she recognized him.

Seymour.

He said, "I need a doctor."

"Do you have a gun?"

He shook his head.

She stopped in front of him.

"Where'd your buddies go?"

"I don't know." He was grunting through the pain and blood was still trickling through his fingers. Sophie unsnapped her handcuffs, knelt down, and popped a bracelet around Seymour's left wrist. The other cuff, she locked to the handrail.

He groaned. "You have to help me."

"Help's coming. Keep pressure on that wound. You'll be fine."

Sophie grabbed Angela's ID badge from her pocket and swiped it through the card reader.

The door buzzed and she shouldered her way through into the blinding illumination of a floodlight.

Started jogging along a walkway between the dark buildings.

She was disoriented—no idea of her location relative to the main entrance—and she couldn't hear a thing over the sound of rain beating down on the grass, the pavement, her head.

She accelerated.

In the distance, she spotted a row of streetlights.

The parking lot.

She was sprinting now, the rain driving into her face, boots streaking through pools of standing water that had collected in the grass.

She broke out from the buildings, crossed a sidewalk, and blitzed into the parking lot. She was panting, years since she'd run this hard.

Wiping rainwater out of her eyes, she spotted the van in the distance. A trio of dark shapes jogged toward it, carrying something wrapped in white.

Sophie reached a gray Honda Accord and took shelter behind it, rain pouring off her face, lungs burning as she gasped for breath.

Where is my backup?

She glanced through the windows.

The van was fifty feet away.

Three men struggled to carry what appeared to be another man over their heads. They looked like errant pallbearers moving across the barren parking lot.

She got to her feet, and over the roof of the Accord, sited down the men and the van.

Water streamed off the slide, the Glock's polymer frame beaded with rain.

It was harder than she had imagined—much harder—summoning her voice.

"Stop! Seattle Police!"

The men didn't flinch, didn't react.

She yelled it again at the top of her voice.

They were almost to the van. In unison, they dropped to their knees and set the man in white on the wet pavement. One of their number rushed forward to the sliding door, fumbling with a set of keys.

His partners turned.

"Get on the ground!" Sophie yelled.

Never saw them draw.

A pair of muzzleflashes bloomed and the windows exploded.

She squeezed off six shots—no precision aiming, just panicked, general direction, not-wanting-to-die chaos fire—and then ducked behind the front passenger door.

The cold, wet pavement soaking through her pants.

Four gunshots echoed off the buildings, the rounds chinking into the metal of the Honda. Her ears still ringing, she peeked over the jagged range of glass sticking up out of the bottom of the door.

Grazer and Vincent had returned to the van where they were helping Talbert lift Moreton off the ground and stow him inside. She drew a bead on one of them, but she didn't trust her aim with Moreton in the mix.

Two of the men disappeared with Moreton into the van and the last one—Grazer?—turned and fired three shots at the Accord. Sophie took cover behind the door again as air rushed out of the front tire on the other side, the car sagging forward and away from her.

She heard the van's sliding passenger door ram shut.

Popped up, double-tapped at Grazer as he rushed around the hood of the van and piled in behind the wheel.

The engine started, and as Sophie ran out from behind the car, the tires spun on pavement for a split second, caught, and then launched the van across the parking lot.

Planting her feet shoulder-width apart, she aimed at the right, rear tire.

It was the only moment since rolling onto the hospital grounds that she'd possessed a shred of self-awareness. She made herself breathe. She saw that micron of space beyond the night sights that she knew was the tire. Saw the white puff of air as the bullet pierced the tread. Saw the van spin out of control. The cavalry arrive. Jim Moreton saved, his kidnappers in cuffs on the ground.

She fired.

She fired again.

And again.

And again and again and again.

The next time she squeezed the trigger, the slide locked back, smoke coiling off the exposed barrel of the Glock.

The van turned hard out of the parking lot, tires fully intact and squealing across the wet road. It straightened and accelerated, the engine winding up, RPMs maxed.

She'd missed.

Seven times.

And now Jim Moreton, father of the man she might possibly love, was going to die.

She stood in the rain, stunned by her failure.

Here came the sirens.

She started running toward her car.

Chapter 39

Grant started down the stairs, the blanket jostling in his arms. He could feel the creature wrapped inside vibrating like a tuning fork. It put out so much body heat that the blanket could have just come out of a dryer.

"What's happening?" Paige asked, a few steps behind him.

"It's ready to leave."

"It told you that?"

He reached the bottom of the stairs and made his way across the foyer to the front door.

"Grant."

He stopped.

"What?"

"Talk to me."

"I have to take it somewhere."

"Where?" she asked.

"I'm not sure yet."

He turned and stepped into his boots. With his free hand, he grabbed the North Face jacket off the coat rack and draped it over his shoulder.

Paige arrived at the bottom of the staircase. She clutched the banister, panic and a profound sadness in her eyes.

"It's in your head now," she said. "You're like the others."

Grant shifted the weight from one arm to the other and looked back at her.

The blankets moved in his arms.

A translucent appendage emerged.

Paige recoiled, placed a foot on the step behind her as Grant covered it back with a loose fold.

"I don't understand it all, but I'm still Grant," he said, though he only half-believed.

"You went upstairs to kill that thing."

"I have to go."

"This is insane. You don't even know what it's telling you to do."

"You're right. But it won't be in your house anymore. It'll be out of your life."

He saw the early shimmer of tears in her eyes.

"What happened in there?" Paige asked.

He looked at her. What could he possibly say? That even though he'd never been a father, he felt like he was holding his child in his arms? That with every passing second, that feeling was growing stronger? On the verge of eclipsing the protective instinct he'd felt toward his own sister when she was five years old and all he had in the world?

"It's not something I can explain," he said. "I just don't have the words."

"I don't understand what's happening."

"Me either."

"So what now?"

"I put this thing in the car and start driving."

Paige released her death-grip on the railing. She wiped her eyes. Her shoulders relaxed.

She went to the rack and grabbed her jacket—a charcoal gray peacoat with wooden toggles.

"We can take my car," she said.

"Excuse me?"

"I'll drive. You navigate."

"Paige, this is my thing now. My burden. You've carried it long enough. You don't have to come."

She put the coat on over her plaid pajamas, stepped into a pair of black Uggs.

"We've had enough of leaving each other, don't you think?"

Excluding two brief excursions that had nearly killed him, it had been almost a day and a half since Grant had been outside, and the feeling of moving down the steps without an onslaught of debilitating pain bordered on surreal. Like walking out of prison. He didn't entirely trust it, still half-expecting the blinding migraine to T-bone him at any moment.

The rain was torrential, huge drops smacking the flagstones beneath Grant's and Paige's feet as they headed toward the sidewalk.

"Where'd you park?" Grant yelled over the rain.

"Around the corner."

They walked up the sidewalk, Grant holding the blanket tightly in his arms, grateful for the warmth.

Turning the corner, they moved alongside the wrought-iron fence.

Paige reached into her pocket.

Up ahead, the car alarm on a black CR-V chirped. Paige jogged ahead and opened the curbside rear passenger door.

Grant ducked in.

She shut him inside.

The car smelled new.

Rain pounding the roof and the windshield.

Paige climbed in behind the wheel, cranked the engine.

"Five-twenty," Grant said.

"Across Lake Washington?"

"Yep."

"That's toward Kirkland. Toward Dad."

"I know."

Paige buckled herself in and put the car into gear. Pulled out of the parking space. There was no one on the street—pedestrian or vehicle. They cruised past rows of streetlamps, rain pouring through the spheres of light.

He blinked and Paige was accelerating up the I-5 onramp, merging onto the empty interstate.

He lost time again.

Falling inward.

Then they were several miles down the road, alone on 520, barreling east across the floating bridge as the toll cameras flashed blue above them.

Grant felt intensely purposeful. As zoned-out and deep as if he were under the influence of a psychotropic drug, and yet still in control of his faculties. The strangest paradox—complete self-ownership but on a new plain of awareness.

As if all his life had been leading toward this moment.

He didn't speak.

Didn't think.

Just clutched the blanket to his chest—was this what it felt like to bring your newborn son home from the hospital?—and watched the sleeping city out his window.

"Grant."

He returned to the moment.

Lake Washington still out the window.

Paige was reaching into the backseat, her phone lighting up in her hand. She said, "It's Sophie."

He took the phone.

"Hello?"

"Grant?"

"Are you with my father?"

"They took him." Sophie was crying—he could hear it in her voice.

"Is he alive?" Grant asked.

"I couldn't ... stop it ... from happening."

"Is he alive?"

"I don't know." She was becoming hysterical. He could barely understand her. "I'll find him, Grant. I swear to you."

"I know you did everything you could. I don't blame you for anything."

"Are you and Paige okay?"

"I have to go now."

"Grant, what's wrong? Are you still at the house? Did something happen? *Grant?*"

He powered off the phone.

Paige said, "What happened?"

"They took Dad."

"Who? My clients?"

"Sophie lost them. They got away."

Paige began to hyperventilate.

"I need you to calm down," Grant said. "You have to get us there safely."

"Explain to me what happened."

"I don't fully understand."

"Then call her back!"

"It doesn't matter, Paige."

"They took our father!"

"Are you still okay to drive me?"

Page relaxed her grip on the steering wheel.

"Yeah."

She settled back into her seat.

"I'm trusting you, Grant."

"Thank you."

"I need to know that you know how this is going to end."

"I don't."

"Then what are you trusting?"

Chapter 40

The sky over the gas station parking lot where Sophie sat with the engine cooling was just beginning to brighten into a flat gray. She ended her fourth and final call to Paige's cell and let her head fall back against the headrest. Like every other attempt, straight to voice mail.

—*Where are you? An APB went out half an hour ago, and a van fitting the description was just spotted in Bothell. I'm on my way. Call me.*

—*Almost to Bothell. Call me.*

—*I'm pulling into the gas station where the van was spotted. Where are you?*

She had gotten the clerk inside to replay the footage—*van pulls up to the pump, glare on the windshield too severe to ID who's at the wheel, but Vincent—unmistakable—exits from the sliding passenger door five seconds later. He walks around the hood of the van and stops in front of the pump where he digs a card out of his wallet and feeds it to the machine. Three unbearable minutes of waiting while he gasses up, the man staring dead into the camera the entire time. Finally, he caps the tank, returns the nozzle, and climbs inside. A few seconds later, the van rolls out of frame.*

From the angle of the camera, it was impossible to tell which direction they had turned as the van left the parking lot, and no amount of coaxing could jog the cashier's memory.

Sophie had spent the next forty-five minutes canvassing the area, checking motel parking lots, restaurants, and drive-thrus, her strategy ultimately disintegrating into blind Hail Mary turns down empty side streets.

She'd finally pulled back into the gas station and parked in the spot where she now sat, staring up at the ceiling of her car as if someone had scrawled the answers there.

Sophie shut her eyes.

The rain had tapered off into drizzle again, padding softly against the windshield.

Her phone rang beside her in her passenger seat.

She grabbed it.

Not Grant.

Officer Silver.

She answered, "Hey, Bobby."

"I'm just leaving the brownstone in Queen Anne."

"And?"

"Nobody home."

Sophie's heart lurched.

"You're sure?"

"Empty as the warm, comfy spot beside my wife where I was soundly sleeping thirty minutes ago."

"Did you go inside?"

"No. Just banged on the front door and then peered through the windows. Lights are on downstairs but it's a ghost town."

Sophie exhaled.

"Thanks, Bobby. I owe you big time for tonight. Apologize to Lynette for me."

For a long beat, all she could hear was the acceleration of Bobby's engine bleeding through the speaker.

She said, "You there, Bobby?"

"You know I got your back, right?"

"I know that."

"There anything you want to tell me?"

She could feel the corners of her mouth beginning to quiver, her eyes blurring with tears. In this moment, there was nothing she wanted more in the world than to tell everything.

"Sophie?"

She squeezed the phone.

Steadied her voice as best she could.

"Everything's fine. Go home, Bobby."

The frequency of passing cars was increasing—early commuters heading toward the interstate to beat the rush into Seattle.

It felt like years since she'd seen her last clear day, one of those rare cloudless beauties when every horizon looms with mountains and the Puget sparkles and Rainier threatens to the south like the badass stratovolcano that it is.

What had she really seen, *really* experienced in Paige's brownstone?

Grant had told her some whacked-out things. He'd certainly acted crazy.

But ...

What had she *actually experienced* that verified a goddamn thing?

A bad dream and a power surge.

That was it.

Hadn't seen any creepy twin girls who wanted to play forever.

No one crawling across the ceiling.

There had been the phone video from Paige's room, but it was just that. A video.

So let's talk about what you did see. Something you could actually write down in a report that wouldn't get you laughed at and fired ...

—Her partner had lied to her repeatedly about his whereabouts and absence.

—When she finally found him, Grant had overpowered her, taken her gun, cuffed her to a banister.

—She'd been held against her will in what was for all intents and purposes a modern-day bordello.

—A good man had died violently more than thirty hours ago in a bathroom upstairs, and her partner, as of yet, had failed to report his death, even to his wife.

—And when the shit really hit the fan with Art and their father at the asylum, brother and sister had vanished.

Yes, things had felt off inside the house, but now, with a little distance and perspective, the cold, dispassionate facts were rising out of the mire. And when it came time to sort things out—the actions of Paige's clients, of Paige and Grant themselves, the death of Don—it was only those facts that would matter.

You covered for them, Sophie.

Lied for them.

And maybe she would've continued to. Maybe she would've extended her partner's credit just a little longer, given him a chance to sort things out ... but for Don.

Don overshadowed all.

Because when you stripped everything away, the simple fact of the matter was that a good man was dead. And his memory, his wife, deserved an accounting.

She scrolled through contacts.

Sorry, Grant.

Pressed dial.

It only rang once, and the voice of the woman who answered sounded a far cry from the person Sophie knew.

All she said was, "Hello?" but it carried the ragged weariness of a soul in torment.

"Rachel?"

"Yes?"

"This is Sophie Benington."

"Are you calling about Don?"

Sophie could feel the tears coming, the emotion dislodging in the center of her chest like a giant piece of ice calving off from her berg of grief.

"I'm afraid I am."

Chapter 41

Dawn.

They were in the clouds, moving along wet pavement, the fir trees rushing past.

Occasionally, he glimpsed a mountain—dark, wet rock, swaths of snow across the higher terrain.

There was no more rain, only mist, but it was thick enough at this elevation to keep the windshield wipers in perpetual motion.

Grant swallowed.

His ears popped.

The engine groaned, the CR-V struggling up the steepest pitch of road so far, the double yellow winding endlessly ahead of them.

His right hand was inside the blanket, as it had been for the last hour, a tiny, warm appendage gripping his pinkie finger. He stared out the window. Saw everything and nothing. A kind of dual consciousness.

All up the mountainsides, the clouds were catching in the branches of the dark, epic trees. Their sharp, clean scent so strong he could smell them through the glass.

Paige watched him in the rearview mirror. He could feel her stare. The intensity of it.

He said, "We're almost there."

She said, "I know."

•••

They turned off of Highway 2.

A gravel road shot ahead through the forest, badly overgrown, but still navigable.

Just ahead, recent tire marks made paths through the undergrowth that peaked up through the loose rock.

They rolled slowly between giant hemlocks, the CR-V tilting and swaying across the uneven ground.

Grant could feel the blanket growing hotter, the shuddering intensifying, its grip around his finger tightening.

It was a minute past six a.m.

In the narrow corridor below the trees, Paige had punched on the high beams.

After a quarter of a mile, they broke out of the forest.

He had come here once since that last family vacation when it had been the four of them. Several years ago, a case had taken him out to Nason Creek, and he'd stopped by the old homestead; driven in as far as the clearing, but he'd never shut the car off, never even gotten out. Just sat in his Crown Vic for five minutes, hands clenched around the steering wheel, knuckles blanching, as if he could steel himself against the storm he'd been fighting all of his life.

So much pain caught. So much joy missed.

And there was no better embodiment than this decrepit place.

The cabin stood in the middle of a small clearing that had become considerably less clear in the years since his last visit.

It was a log-frame house, single story, with a steeply-sloping roof of rusted tin.

The front porch was covered, and even though the light was bad, Grant could make out Vincent, Talbert, and Grazer sitting in the rocking chairs.

Paige pulled into the grass beside the black van and cut the engine.

"Are we safe?" Paige asked.

"Why don't you wait in the car for a minute," Grant said.

He opened the door and stepped out.

It was freezing, the forest dripping, everything wet.

The hemlocks leaned in above them.

Their smell like a time machine.

He saw Paige—a little girl—running across the sunlit clearing on a summer day. Their mother reading on the porch. His father chopping wood. Their own private oasis.

The smell of Talbert's cigarette dragged him back to this cold, gray morning.

Grant moved through the waist-high weeds and stopped at the foot of the steps.

Talbert stood.

Dropped his cigarette on the rotting wood of the porch.

Stamped it out.

Vincent and Grazer rose to their feet, the chairs rocking in the sudden wake of their absence. Their suits mud-stained, torn in places, sodden. Dried blood down the front of Talbert's pinstripe shirt.

Grant said, "Where is he?"

"Inside."

Grant nodded and Talbert moved across the porch, came down the steps with his cohorts in tow.

He stopped in front of Grant.

Put a hand on both shoulders, a smile slowly spreading across his face.

"We're glad you made it," Talbert said. "It's almost over."

Pats on Grant's back as the others passed.

Talbert released his shoulders and continued on.

Grant turned and watched them climb into the van.

Vincent in the driver seat.

Grazer rode shotgun and Talbert disappeared through the sliding door.

The engine cranked and the van circled through the clearing and headed back toward the road.

A hundred feet in, it vanished into the darkness between the hemlocks, nothing but a pair of brake lights dwindling into the gloom.

Paige got out of the CR-V and walked over.

"What'd he say?"

"That it's almost over."

Grant heard the distant revving of the van's engine as it pulled out onto the highway. Within ten seconds, it was out of earshot. The only note left was the wind moving through the top of the forest and the hemlock branches groaning against its force.

Grant and Paige climbed the steps to the porch.

There were beer bottles and cans strewn across the floorboards. Empty packs of cigarettes. Rounds of Skoal dipping tobacco. Old and shriveled condoms. Spent twelve gauge shells. A Penthouse magazine, waterlogged and faded.

Their old vacation home had become a Friday night hangout for teenagers from the surrounding towns.

The front door stood ajar and sagging, attached to the frame by its lowest hinge.

Grant reached for it with his free hand.

It swung inward, arcing toward the floor until it came to a scraping halt after two feet.

He glanced at Paige. "Hang back a second."

Grant turned sideways with the blanket and stepped through the narrow opening.

The air inside was redolent of pine and smoke and mildew.

There was a small fire in the hearth, illuminating the room with a pulsating light that made the rafters cast a ribcage of shadows on the vaulted ceiling.

Graffiti covered the walls.

Dates and genitalia.

Names preceded by *fuck* or *love*.

In the back corner, rotten railing separated the rest of the room from what had been the kitchenette. It was now unrecognizable, buried under the debris of a failed roof, cabinets and counters long-since disintegrated under seasons of rain and snow. Nothing to suggest its prior status beyond a doorless refrigerator peppered with buckshot.

Grant walked over to the fireplace, the glass-littered floor crunching under his boots.

Two generations' worth of faded Bud Light cans lined the railroad tie that served as a mantle. It was the only place in the cabin that seemed to command some level of order and respect, if nothing more than a nod by the collective consciousness of those who came here to the passage of time.

He stared at the bare wall above the mantle where a painting of his mother's—an acrylic of the pond out back—used to hang three decades ago. He could still see the nail hole in the cracking drywall that the picture frame's wire had rested upon.

He reached up and touched it, then turned and leveled his gaze on the two doors in the wall across the room.

The first led into the bedroom he and Paige had shared as children, but Grant made his way through the detritus of a thousand Friday nights toward the second.

Their parent's room.

He pushed it open, the hinges screeching.

Could no longer feel the heat of the fire, and its glow didn't come close to lighting these walls whose wood-paneling had buckled and peeled like the diseased bark of a dying birch tree.

He stepped inside.

All the furniture was gone save for a single mattress pushed into the corner.

His father lay on it, writhing in a straightjacket.

Grant crossed the room and lowered himself slowly to his knees. When he set the blanket on the filthy mattress, his father became perfectly still, lying on his stomach, his back heaving as he panted for breath.

There were four straps going across the back of the straightjacket. Grant reached over and unbuckled them.

Then he turned his father onto his back.

His old man's eyes were huge. They stared at the ceiling, blinking several times a second.

Grant pulled his arms out of the straightjacket sleeves and arranged them at his sides.

He was coming out of himself, out of that deep well. Felt strange to be in proximity to his father, unrestrained and unmedicated. More so to see him lying still, not thrashing around.

Grant unwrapped the blanket, the heat becoming more evident with each layer.

As he peeled back the last fold, he could feel it lapping at his face like a hot breeze.

Its eyes seemed to catch light that wasn't even in the room. They had changed—now infinitely-faceted, and with the wet sheen of a river-polished stone.

His father's respirations slowed.

Grant lifted the creature, set it on his old man's chest like a newborn.

As it began to sink into him, he turned away and walked out of the room.

Paige was by the fire, holding her hands to the heat.

The sound of the door shutting pulled her attention to Grant.

He moved across the room and stood beside her.

"Is Dad in there?" she asked.

"Yeah."

"Did they hurt him?"

"No."

"And he's in there ... with *it*?"

He nodded.

"Why?"

"I have no idea."

"Just doing what you're told, huh?" She didn't say it maliciously.

"Something like that."

"God, it feels so weird to be here."

Grant went to the only piece of furniture in the room—a sofa covered in shredded upholstery.

The springs groaned and the cushion released a mushroom cloud of dust as he sat.

He swatted it away.

Old chimes clanged on the back porch.

The walls of the cabin strained against a blast of wind.

Being indoors somehow made the cold feel colder.

Paige looked around the cabin.

"Haven't thought about this place in ages," she said. "It's like something from someone else's life. I do love what they've done with the place."

Grant glanced at the ceiling.

The names *Mike + Tara* stared down at him in faded, billowy letters.

"I always thought the ceiling was so much higher," Grant said. "I think I could touch the rafters now if I jumped."

For a long time, neither of them spoke. Grant tried to hear any noises coming from the room, but the only sound in the cabin was the brittle crackling of the fire. He couldn't shake the feeling that he was slowly waking up, the last several hours steadily descending into a subconscious fog like the memory of a dream, or a nightmare. The taste of it fading. Fragments gone missing or out of sequence. The flat-out strangeness of this moment, and all that had come before, beginning to register.

At first, he thought it was the work of the wind—something blown loose and knocking against the cabin. But as it continued, he identified the noise as footsteps on weakened floorboards.

The door to what had been their parents' room creaked open.

Paige had already turned away from the fire.

She drew in a sharp breath.

James Moreton stood barefoot in the doorway wearing the same light blue pajama bottoms and button-down shirt he had been drugged and put to bed in by the hospital staff. It looked as though he'd attempted to smooth down the chaos of his hair, but most of it was still frazzled, sticking out to one side in wild tangles of white. A boney shoulder peaked through where the shirt slipped down.

Standing under his own steam, Jim Moreton looked impossibly frail.

A lifetime in the acute ward had aged him well beyond his fifty-nine years.

Grant stood up.

Paige said, "Daddy?"

Jim was looking right at them. Even from across the room, Grant could see the bright clarity in his father's eyes.

And their focus—

His father hadn't looked him in the eye with anything approaching recognition since he was a child.

Jim smiled, said, "My children." He looked at Grant. "You did great, kiddo. Come on back now."

It was like being pulled from deep water. Grant's ear popped, and he was suddenly keenly aware that he was standing in the old family cabin with his sister nearby and his father upright and alert in the doorway. His recollection of Paige's room, the car ride, unwrapping the creature—it all retained its vivid detail, but held no immediacy. As if the last three hours were something he'd seen on a TV show.

Jim took a wobbly step forward but then clutched the doorframe.

Grant rushed over and grabbed his father under his arms, kept him upright. He could feel the tremor in his old man's legs—atrophied muscles already maxed. He reeked of the hospital.

Jim said, "Been a little while since I stood on these feet."

Two days of strange happenings could not compete with the shock of hearing his father speak. Not groans or sighs or the ravings of a man whose mind was gone, but the sound of his actual voice powered by lucid thought. It contained the soft, raspy element of an instrument that hadn't seen use in decades.

"Son, would you help me over to the sofa?"

"Yes, sir."

Grant let his old man lean against him for support. He was light as paper. They took slow and shuffling steps together, Grant doing his best to guide him around the broken glass.

When they reached the sofa, Grant eased his father back onto the center cushion and took a seat beside him.

"Hi, princess." Jim was smiling up at Paige. He patted the cushion beside him. "Come here. I want to be near you."

She walked over and sat with him, wrapped her arms around his neck.

"Don't cry," he whispered as she buried her face into his shoulder. "You have absolutely no reason to cry."

Jim looked down at his hands. Turned them over. They were long and gnarled, the joints swollen, nails trimmed to nothing.

"How old am I?" he asked.

Grant answered, "Fifty-nine."

Jim laughed. "So this is what old age looks like. God, I could use a smoke."

For a moment, the cabin clung to the stiffest silence.

Nothing but Paige's muffled sobs.

Even the wind had died away.

"Dad," Grant finally said, "I've been visiting you every two weeks for the last twenty years. They keep you drugged and restrained. The few times they haven't you've injured others and yourself. They said your brain suffered so much trauma in the accident that you barely retained cognitive function. Said you'd never recover."

"I've been gone," Jim said.

"I know."

"No." His father's lips curled into a small smile that Grant hadn't seen in thirty-one years. "You don't."

Jim raised his arms and put them around his children, pulled them both in close.

He said, "You cannot imagine what it feels like to touch you again. To speak to you and hear your voice. To see the color of your eyes. I've seen so much, but nothing can touch this."

"What do you mean you've seen so much?" Grant said. "You've been confined to a psychiatric hospital since the accident."

Jim shook his head.

Again with that sly little smile.

"I've been everywhere, son."

Paige lifted her head off Jim's shoulder.

"What are you talking about, Daddy?"

"How much do you kids remember about the night of the accident?"

Paige said, "I was five, Grant was seven. He probably remembers more than I do. For me, it's just a few images. Light coming through the windshield. The guardrail. And then after … you not moving."

"I remember a lot of it," Grant said. "Most clearly talking to Paige when the car was upside down and she was hurt and scared."

"I'm so sorry I wasn't there to help you," Jim said. "Not only for that night, but for every moment of your lives leading up to this one."

"It's okay," Grant said. "You were hurt. There was nothing you could do."

"I wasn't hurt that night."

"Of course you were. I can rattle off ten symptoms and behavioral manifestations associated with your traumatic brain injury."

"What you visited in the hospital wasn't me. It was just my hardware."

"What are you talking about?" Paige asked.

Jim sighed.

"That night, we were on our way here. It was late. I was tired. Lights blinded me—I thought it was a semi. I over-steered, took us through the guardrail. We were in the air forever. You guys weren't screaming and I remember thinking how strange that was. I guess you didn't understand what was happening. We hit the side of the mountain and rolled and rolled and rolled.

"When we finally stopped, I knew I was bad-off. I could feel my ribs in places they shouldn't be. Breathing was excruciating. I couldn't move. Neither of you were making noise in the backseat and the rearview was busted so I didn't even know if you guys were alive. I called out to you, but you didn't answer. I just hung there from the seat and cried. I don't know for how long.

"At some point, I realized I had missed the end of the game, and somehow I convinced myself that if the Phillies had won, you kids were alive. I can't explain it. It just made perfect sense in the moment. I'm sure the blood loss had gone to my head. So I started praying, 'Dear God, let the Phillies win.' Not 'Dear God, save us' or 'Dear God, please don't let my kids be hurt.' The Phillies were our ticket out of there.

"The pain grew unbearable—the physical, the psychological, worrying about the two of you. I remember seeing a light coming through the trees. At first, I thought it was our rescue party, but the light kept getting brighter. It wasn't a solitary beam or even a collection of them, but all-encompassing. It intensified until everything—the car, the trees—was bathed in a blinding white radiance. My pain vanished, and everything I am—my consciousness, the unbreakable essence you would think of as a soul—was taken."

A long, breathless beat of silence.

The fire had burned itself out—the blackened log venting smoke up the chimney and the early morning cold flooding in, driving out what little warmth the flames had given.

"At first, I thought I had died. My spirit cut loose, adrift in the emptiness of space. But then …" he drew a trembling breath, "… those first moments. The stars moving. Inconceivable velocity. The knowledge that I wasn't alone.

"They took me through the pinnacle of a young nebula whose light won't touch earth for another million years. A spire of dust and hydrogen gas four light years tall.

"We traveled, my guides intent on my reaction to things. To understanding my attachments—the constraints of emotion—which they perceived as weakness. Barriers to advancement. These beings were pure mind, stripped of emotion, evolved beyond the need to wrap themselves in matter. They were benevolent, but their intelligence was terrifying. They exist outside the jurisdiction of space and time.

"I saw stars born. I watched them die. I saw things that will never have names in our lifetimes. That Shakespeare and Van Gogh couldn't have begun to do justice. Sun-sized worlds patchworked with bioelectric grids more intricate than the human eye. I witnessed the shockwave from a supernova destroy a solar system, and then stood on the surface of what was left—a neutron star no bigger than Manhattan. They took me to the brink of an event horizon, let me gaze into the abyss while it devoured a sun. Even as I say the words, your mind attempts to draw a picture, but it can't. Whatever you imagine fails.

"They wanted to purge my humanity with the sheer grandeur of things, but it persisted. The resilience of my hope and love and fear fascinated them. They asked what I most wanted to experience. I told them ..." here, his voice broke, "... my wife. They took me to a place where your mother never died. Where we never went off the side of a mountain. Where we never knew separation. You both brought your children to this cabin. I chased them through the meadow. We swam in the pond. I got drunk with your wife, Grant. And with your husband, Paige. We all sat on the front porch of a summer evening and filled this clearing with our laughter. I was holding Julia's hand. To breathe the air of a world where our family thrived, where we were happy ... it was something ... and I could have stayed, I could've stayed forever ... but it wasn't mine.

"No matter where they took me, no matter what I saw, my heart was here. This cabin. This world. This reality. The two of you. They couldn't grasp it. They'd chosen me for this revelation. The universe unveiled. They had undocked my mind from this frail shell so I could become like them—pure conscious energy—and I wanted to come back."

"Why?" Grant asked.

"Why." His father laughed. "'Why?' asks a man who has never had a child. Because I'm tethered to you. To both of you, as you exist right here. You're the only thing that's real to me. That gives my existence meaning."

Grant motioned toward the bedroom.

"What's in there?"

"Nothing now. I absorbed it."

"What *was* in there?"

"Returning, inhabiting my physical form—" Jim opened his hands and stared at them "—this antiquated piece of engineering ... was an uncertain proposition. It's not as simple as just plugging back into my old body. That thing in there was created to serve as a conduit, a flash drive for lack of a better analogy. But it needed to make physical contact with my body to effect the download."

"What if you'd been killed in the wreck?"

"They would have taken me just the same. I just wouldn't have been able to come back and make contact with the two of you." He turned to Paige and patted her knee. "My darling, you wore that same look on your face when you were five. I see you've not let it gather dust."

"What look, Daddy?"

"Like I'm bullshitting you."

"You're saying that was you under my bed?"

"Something went wrong on my return. It was my fault. I let myself get drawn to your energy instead of my shell at the hospital. I came to consciousness in your backyard. That thing is barely mobile, ill-equipped for earth's gravitational and atmospheric demands. It was all I could do to crawl up the steps of your brownstone. I hid under your bed while you slept. The weeks I spent there, I was slowly dying. Desperate to find some way to reunite with my earth form."

"I thought you were a ghost. Or a demon. Do you have any idea of the hell you put us through?"

"I'm so sorry. I didn't mean to cause you pain. I couldn't communicate with you, Paige. At least not like this."

"But you had this incredible power. There were times you were in my head. In my dreams. I couldn't leave the house."

"I was trying to talk to you. I couldn't *let* you leave. I needed you. I reached out to you the only way I could, but it was awkward—like riding a bicycle backward and blindfolded. In that form, the one Grant carried in here, I was so weak, so vulnerable, and running out of time."

"What did you do to those men?" she asked.

"Think of it as installing a program. You see why I needed them."

"Will they have any memory of this?"

"I imagine their experience will be similar to Grant's." Jim glanced at his son.

"Like waking after a dream," Grant said.

"Exactly. And as time passes, the memory of it will fade away."

"You had them break into a hospital," Paige said. "There will be—"

"Consequences?" He smiled. "Are you really going to ask me if I'm concerned that four men who have been using my little girl will have some explaining to do? I would've done anything to be with the two of you again."

"A good man died," Grant said. "Don."

"I know, and I'm sick about it. The others were vulnerable. Their guards were down when I broke inside their minds."

"What do you mean?"

"The region of the brain behind the left eye—the lateral orbitofrontal cortex—shuts down during orgasm. This is our center for reason and behavioral control. It gave me an opening."

Paige blushed deeply and stared at the floor.

Jim's eyes darkened. "I don't know what happened with your friend. He was suddenly in the room. He saw me. I tried to make him leave, but I could barely get inside. It was just a handhold, but it devastated him. None of this has been easy or gone like I'd hoped. But we're here now, aren't we? Together again."

"You still have this power?" Grant asked.

"Only to an extent. I'm still adjusting to life back in this skin. It's awkward."

Paige held her head in her hands.

Still staring at the floor.

"But how do we know?" she asked.

"Know what?"

"That this is really you? Our father. We've been through hell the last two days. For me, it's been even longer. Scared out of my mind. Thinking I'm going crazy. And then suddenly this?"

"I know it's difficult, sweetheart. I'm so sorry. But you know it's me, don't you? Can't you feel it? Haven't you, in some way that maybe you only now recognize, known it all along?"

"Assuming everything you've said is true, what did you think? That after all this time, all you say you experienced, you could just come back and it would all be okay again? You were gone for thirty years."

"And yet to me it was only a month. I didn't know what to expect, Paige. That's the truth, and I didn't care. I just wanted to be with the two of you. To make things right for us again. I know it's been hard, darling." He reached out, touched his daughter's face with a trembling hand. "This isn't the life I wanted for you."

Tears rolled down her cheeks, but she didn't look away from him this time.

"You could've been anything you wanted, Paige."

He turned to Grant. "And you're coming apart on the inside, son. I felt it under the bed. Your rage. Your loneliness. The urge you sometimes have to just end it. You're still that little boy and girl to me, and now to see you both grown and struggling like this … it kills me."

"It hasn't been easy," Grant said. "We had no one."

"So what now?" Paige asked. "As you say, nothing went as planned. We're in a big mess here, Daddy."

"I know, but I have a way to fix things."

The sound had been slowly building in Grant's subconscious, and for the first time, he was aware of its presence.

Jim had started to say something, but he stopped when Grant rose to his feet.

"What's wrong?" Paige asked.

Grant moved quickly across the room to one of the windows that looked out across the porch into the meadow.

The sound was the crunch of tires rolling over gravel.

Sophie's TrailBlazer emerged out of the forest and moved through the clearing toward the cabin. A few seconds behind, he spotted a white Chevy Caprice topped with a light bar.

Didn't even need to see the emblem on the doors.

"What is it, Grant?" Paige asked again.

"Sophie. And she's brought along a Statie."

Chapter 42

Loose gravel pinged the undercarriage of Sophie's Trailblazer as it slid to a stop next to a black CR-V.

A derelict cabin loomed straight ahead, surrounded by hemlocks.

Front windows busted out.

Too dark to tell if anyone was inside.

Sophie killed the engine and watched the Caprice approach in the rearview mirror. When she'd asked for backup, she'd envisioned more force than one lonely Statie. Then again, what could you expect in the sticks?

The Caprice pulled up beside her.

She grabbed a fresh magazine from the glove box and climbed out.

Slammed her door as the trooper stepped out of his cruiser.

Crisp blue suit.

Flat-brimmed hat.

Tall, rail-thin, blinding smile.

"Sophie Benington," Sophie said. "So it's just you?"

"Trooper Todd. But Bob's plenty. What's the dealio?"

"There was supposed to be a black van here. Three men abducted a fifty-nine-year-old patient from a psychiatric hospital in Kirkland. He's violent. They brought him here was my understanding."

"In the black van?"

"Exactly."

"And how did you come by this information?"

"One of the other suspects called me when they arrived. That's her car."

"What'd she do?"

"I'll have to get back to you on that."

"We gonna go say hello?"

Sophie studied the cabin.

Curls of smoke plumed out of the chimney and up into the branches.

"I am."

"I got a shotgun in my trunk."

"This isn't gonna end that way."

"No offense, ma'am, but that's not always up to us."

"Why don't you go around back. Make sure the van's not there. Cover the back door."

"When do I bust in?"

"You don't. Not unless you see my gun. We clear on that, Bob?"

He released the button snap on his holster, grinned.

"It was a joke."

Bob high-stepped his way through the overgrowth and disappeared around the corner of the cabin.

Sophie thumbed off the snap on her holster and started toward the covered porch.

Mist was forming across the clearing.

She'd been drive-off-the-side-of-the-road tired just moments ago, but now she was fully awake, all systems go.

As she climbed the steps onto the porch, she remembered Grant telling her about this place. It wasn't the rose-tinted family retreat she'd expected. Or the weekend fixer-upper Grant had played it off as. If it hadn't been in the middle of nowhere, the county would have condemned it years ago.

The front door stood open a half-inch, but she knocked anyway, her palm resting on her Glock.

"Seattle Police."

She heard footsteps approaching.

They stopped on the other side, but the door didn't open.

"Sophie?"

He sounded so tired.

"It's me, Grant. Everyone okay?"

"We're fine. How'd you find this place?"

"Who's in there with you?" she asked through the door.

"Just the three of us—Paige, me, my father."

"What about our other friends?"

"Gone."

"Gone?"

"Yeah, they left a little while ago."

"Would you open the door please?"

Nothing happened.

"Grant."

The door swung open, but it caught on the floor and stopped after only a foot.

Grant looked burnt-out, confused, on edge.

The dim interior trembled in the firelight behind him. Sophie craned her neck to see inside, but he blocked her line of sight.

"Gonna invite me in?" Sophie asked.

Grant took a step back.

She squeezed through the opening.

Eyes slow to adjust.

Paige by the hearth.

Old man who was a dead ringer for Seymour's receipt portrait sitting on a disgusting couch.

"This your father?" she asked.

"Yeah. Hey, Dad, meet my partner, Sophie Benington."

Jim Moreton said, "A pleasure."

"Are you injured, sir?"

Jim shook his head.

"I was at the hospital," she said. "I tried to stop those men from taking you. I'm sorry I couldn't."

"It's quite all right. I'm with my children now. How could things get any better?"

"Your condition isn't exactly what I expected," she said.

"He's had a remarkable recovery," Grant said.

"I'm sorry, I'm just confused. Those four men kidnapped you from the hospital just to bring you back to the old family cabin. Didn't harm you in any way. And once they delivered you here ... they just *left*?"

Grant said, "Sophie, relax—"

"I'm all done relaxing. I'm ready for answers now."

She moved past Grant into the gloom of the cabin, fixed her stare on Paige, said, "You called me here, honey, said—"

Grant fired a look at his sister.

"—you were scared. That the van was here, and you didn't know what was going to happen. You asked me to come. I came. So could you or somebody at least extend me the courtesy of explaining what the fuck is going on?"

Paige said, "Grant, I'm sorry, I didn't know what was waiting for us in this cabin. You weren't talking to me. Those men were here. I didn't know what else to do."

Grant turned back to Sophie.

"I wish she hadn't done that."

"That's all you got for me, partner?"

"I wouldn't know how to begin ..."

She'd been simmering since her epiphany in Bothel, but with that, she felt it all boil over.

"You asked me to trust you. I did. Now Art's in the hospital with a concussion. Seymour's injured. I've been shot at. You *kidnapped* me. And Don ..." She felt a tremor enter her voice, steadied it. "Just so you know, I called Rachel. Forensics is at Paige's house right now."

Grant's jaw had gone slack.

"How is she?" he asked.

"How do you think?"

"I'm glad you called her. So ... what? You're here to arrest me?"

"I came first and foremost to make sure you and Paige were safe."

"And after that?"

"To make sure you do the right thing."

"Which is ..."

"Let me bring you in."

"Bring me in." Grant smiled. "And how exactly do you see *that* playing out?"

"I don't know. It doesn't matter. People are dead. Hurt. Missing loved ones."

"Face the music time, huh?"

"Tell the truth. Tell your story."

"Nobody wants to hear my story. I've sat in that interview room for thousands of hours. I can't ever remember wanting to hear someone's story, whatever that even means."

"Grant—"

"I wanted to hear something that would help me make a case. You look me in the eye and tell me I'm wrong."

She couldn't.

He continued, "Our job is not about finding the truth. We want someone we can hand to the DA so they can throw them under the bus. Order restored. Citizenry comforted. I know how this will go down, and so do you."

Grant looked over her shoulder through the space between the door and the doorframe. Of course he'd seen the highway patrol cruiser.

She said, "I know you've been through a lot. I know you've seen things that don't make any sense. I don't even dispute what you've said. But it's time. You know that, don't you? And don't you also know that I will do everything in my power to support you?"

Grant looked at Paige, at his father.

"I want this to be over as much as you do," he said.

"Then let's end it."

"Not happening."

Everyone in the room turned to Paige.

She stepped toward Sophie, away from the hearth. "Walk me through this, Sophie. You show up at the precinct with the three of us in tow. We roll up to the front desk where some tired kid who drew the short straw is half-asleep because it's Saturday morning. He looks up from his Sudoku puzzle and sees you standing there with three suspects in handcuffs. Are we in cuffs? I don't know how this looks in your head. And then Grant steps forward and says, 'I'm here to turn myself in for the crime of' ... what? What does he confess to? What's he guilty of?"

"Nobody said he, or you, or your father are guilty of anything."

"Then why are we with you?"

"Because a man died. In your house. Because shit happened that has to be answered for."

"What if there *are* no answers? At least none that fit neatly into your playbook?"

"Like I just told your brother, you will have my full support."

Paige was still moving toward Sophie, now reaching into her gray coat.

"I'm sorry," Paige said, "but that's just not good enough for my family."

It was the last thing Sophie had expected, and she was utterly unprepared to react.

One second Paige.

The next second Paige with a gun pointed at her face.

Grant spoke first.

"Paige—"

"She thinks you did it. Or I did."

"Did what?"

"Killed Don."

"Of course she doesn't think that. Put the gun down."

"I certainly don't think that," Sophie said, her heart rate escalating, the back of her throat threatening to close.

"I don't believe you."

Grant caught Sophie's eye. "Please don't do anything. Just give me a minute to shut this down."

He took a step toward Paige.

"We're leaving, Grant."

"Paige—"

"I'm done. Two weeks a prisoner in my own goddamn home to have it end like this? To be treated like a criminal?"

"Put it down."

"I didn't do anything wrong."

Jim Moreton had begun the long, painful journey to his feet.

He said, "Not this way, Paigy. It's my fault."

"Stop it, Daddy. Grant, go take her gun away from her," Paige said.
"Paige, you draw down on law enforcement, you get shot. Put—"
Sophie saw it a split second before everything went to hell.
Everyone frozen.
A tableau of ruination.
Grant intense, lips together forming the P in "put" and leaning toward his sister, already on the balls of his feet, like he might be on the verge of making a play to stop this.
Jim standing by the sofa, eyes on Paige.
And Sophie herself, tongue grazing the roof of her mouth as she began to scream the word "no" because of what she had just glimpsed out of the corner of her eye—a tall, slim streak of blue standing in the kitchen behind the muzzle flash of a Smith & Wesson M&P40.
Sophie was too late.
Paige still had the gun trained on the center of her chest, eyes averted to Grant, and her face just beginning to screw up in pain as the bullet punched through a rib on her right side.
The sound of the trooper's gunshot filled the cabin.
She smelled gun smoke.
Paige dropped her gun and stumbled sideways.
Her legs buckled.
The trooper screaming at everyone to lay down, spread out their arms.
Paige sat on the floor, her eyes narrowed, a perplexed expression expanding across her face like she was trying to come to terms with what had just happened.
Grant knelt beside his sister. He was saying her name over and over as she lay across the rotting hardwood, eyes open, blood already beginning to pool beneath her, a line of it running a meandering course over the uneven floor toward Sophie.
She hadn't drawn her gun.
Hadn't moved.
Todd started across the cabin toward the chaos, pushing Jim Moreton back down onto the sofa as he passed.
There was a lot of blood.
Too much.

Oh God.

The trooper coming around the sofa.

Screaming at Grant to get down, screaming he was about to get shot like his sister.

Grant's arm came up.

This time, she saw it happening. What was about to happen. Could have stopped it. Maybe. No. For sure. She could have stopped it by shooting Grant. She eased her Glock an inch up out of her holster, finger in the trigger guard, but she didn't draw.

Just stood there watching as Grant shot the trooper and charged, crashing into him like the vengeance of God.

She did nothing.

Not as Grant straddled the trooper.

Not as he beat his face in with the butt of Paige's revolver.

Three devastating blows.

But he didn't kill him.

Grant struggled onto his feet, his face dotted with blood.

He turned and stared her down.

She thought she was dead, but still she didn't pull.

Jim Moreton already struggling to move around the sofa to his daughter, and when Sophie blinked, Grant was at his sister's side again.

Paige was moaning and he was telling her everything would be okay but there was so much blood.

Grant lifted Paige in his arms.

Sophie heard herself say, "I'm so sorry."

She felt out-of-body.

Immoveable.

She had responded to the fear at the psychiatric hospital, but this was something else entirely.

Paige shot.

A trooper shot.

She was paralyzed.

Too much to process.

Grant was standing now, holding his sister, blood running down his arm and dripping off his elbow onto the floor.

He said something to his father that Sophie missed completely.

She called his name, and for a split second, he looked at her, his eyes so troubled, so distant.

She said, "Let me help."

"Either shoot me or get out of my way."

He pushed past her.

Ripped the door open a few more inches, worked his way through the opening and out onto the porch.

Jim Moreton shuffled after him.

They were already climbing into the car by the time Sophie stepped onto the front porch—Grant in back with Paige, his father struggling to install himself behind the steering wheel.

The engine cranked and roared, tires slinging gravel as Jim whipped the CR-V around and floored it down the road into the trees.

Sophie sat down on the weathered steps.

Her hands shook so badly she could barely pull the phone out of her jacket.

A single bar of 3G.

Her voice sounded so calm, so even making the report. Like she was giving her social security number to her credit card company.

"Do you know where the suspects are going?" the dispatcher asked.

"A hospital I would assume."

"One moment ... Closest is in Leavenworth. It's a level five trauma facility. Thirty-five miles east of your location. I'll alert the local police department."

"Thank you."

"And I can tell them you're en route?"

"Yes."

She slipped back into the cabin and checked on Trooper Todd. He was still unconscious, but there was very little blood—the bullet had just grazed him.

Back outside, she hustled down the steps toward her car.

On some level of consciousness, she was becoming aware that everything about her life had just changed. That from this moment forward she would be a different person. That her only hope of survival lay in finding a way to live with the fact that she had utterly failed everyone in that cabin and probably cost Paige her life.

She should've stopped the trooper.

She should've stopped Grant.

She sped down the one-lane road between the hemlocks.

Turned out onto the highway.

Accelerated through the freezing fog.

Her eyes kept filling up with tears and she kept blinking them away.

The fir trees looked like somber ghosts streaming past on the shoulder of the road, and she couldn't see anything beyond three hundred feet.

The road was climbing now.

The fog thickening.

She punched on the headlights.

The clock read a little past seven a.m., but it didn't feel like morning.

It didn't feel like any time she had ever known.

Her phone vibrated.

She didn't answer.

Her ears popped.

She steered through switchbacks and there were reefs of dirty snow on the sides of the road that grew taller the higher she climbed.

The road straightened out.

One last burst of optimism and purpose.

She was going to Leavenworth. Grant would be there. Paige was going to be okay. She would do what she had to, and no one else would get hurt.

She was nearing the crest of the pass when she saw it. Her foot came off the gas pedal, and she brought her TrailBlazer to a stop in the middle of the road.

"Oh, God," she said. "Please, no."

Chapter 43

The CR-V barreled through the overgrowth while Grant cradled his sister's head in his lap. His father could still handle a car, hooking it around potholes and dead logs while the meager headlights illuminated a solid wall of fog that was always just ahead of them.

Jim called back, "How far's Leavenworth?"

"Forty-five minutes," Grant said, dropping Paige's phone on the seat.

"We'll make it in half the time. And they have a hospital?"

"Barely."

The headlights dipped suddenly as the SUV bottomed out with a sharp metallic scrape.

Paige's head lifted and fell back into his lap.

She moaned, clutching her side.

"Sorry, sweetheart," Jim said. "Didn't catch that one in time."

Grant could see the worried creases above his father's eyes in the rearview mirror.

"How we doing back there?" Jim asked.

"We're doing great," Grant said.

Paige mouthed, "Liar. It really hurts."

"I know."

"I can barely stand it."

He held her hand and let her squeeze it.

The trip back to the highway took only half as long as the drive in.

Soon, they were speeding east on smooth pavement.

Grant pushed his fingers through Paige's hair.

She stared up at him, cheeks pale, eyes heavy. Her skin felt cool and clammy.

"I'm sorry," she said, her voice just a whisper now.

"Don't. Just relax. Everything's gonna be fine."

"I made you hurt someone."

"That man shot my sister. He got off easy."

Paige's smile showed dark-red blood between her teeth.

Grant's stomach tightened.

A liver hit.

"Are you cold?"

She nodded.

He slipped out of his North Face and draped it over her.

They rode on.

Climbing.

Paige's breathing growing faster, more shallow. Beads of sweat forming on her face.

Her eyes had become slivers of white.

"Stay with me," Grant said, squeezing her hand.

She gasped and cut loose a rattling cough.

Red foam appeared at the corners of her mouth.

Her lips moved.

"What was that?" Grant brought his ear so close to her mouth he could hear the bloody vibrato in her lungs.

She drew a tiny breath, let it escape in the smallest whisper: "Bad sister."

The words detonated inside of him.

Grant brushed a few strands of hair away from her face.

"Stop it."

He could feel her blood soaking through his pants. There was too much of it.

Grant looked up.

"Hey."

Caught his father's eyes in the rearview mirror.

They were hauling ass around a sharp turn, the tires just beginning to screech.

"How much longer, Dad?"

"I don't know. Twenty? Twenty-five?"

"We're gonna be pushing it."

Jim's eyes took on a shadow. He focused back on the road.

Grant looked down at his sister.

He smiled through a sheet of tears.

She said, "I heard what you just said."

"I'm sorry."

"It doesn't hurt much anymore."

"That's good."

"I'm thirsty."

"We'll find some water for you."

"Everything looks grey. And I think … that might be the end coming. I can hardly see you, Grant."

"I'm right here, Paige."

"I'm thirsty."

"I'm so glad it was you," he said.

"What?"

"Can you hear me?"

It was a splinter of a nod.

"I know we hurt each other, but I wouldn't have traded you for anything. Do you know that? I need you to know it in your heart."

The edges of her mouth curled.

He leaned down and kissed her forehead.

Jim said, "Grant."

"Yeah?"

"How we doing?"

"She's bleeding to death, Dad. We're not gonna make it."

Grant looked up, saw a new intensity enter his father's eyes.

Jim Moreton said, "There's another way."

Chapter 44

There was a distant squeaking sound, but otherwise the world stood silent.

The highway was empty.

Streamers of fog swept across the pavement.

Sophie drifted over the double yellow to the other side of the road. Doesn't mean anything, she told herself. This could have happened two days ago. Two weeks ago.

On the shoulder, her boots crunched through a crust of blackened snow.

She climbed carefully over the ragged metal and stared down the side of the mountain.

Her breath caught.

An upslope breeze carried the strong scent of gasoline.

Several hundred feet down the mountain, barely visible through the trees and the fog, she spotted Paige's CR-V. The vehicle had come to rest on its backend, the undercarriage propped and teetering against a fir tree, its headlights still blasting twin tubes of light up through the fog.

The squeaking she'd heard was the sound of one of the front wheels, still turning.

Steam or smoke poured out of the crumpled hood.

She counted four bare spots on the snowy hill where the car had struck ground, scoured out the snowpack, and flipped.

"Grant!" Her voice echoed off invisible mountains. *"Can anyone hear me?"*

She dialed 911 and then started down.

The slope was steep, at least thirty degrees, and a good two or three feet of snow covered the ground, the tops of evergreen saplings just poking through.

She descended as fast as she could, but she kept falling, and the snow was going down her boots with every step, her clothes and hair becoming powdered with snow.

The wheel had stopped turning by the time she closed in on the CR-V and the stench of gas was potent. The snow wasn't as deep in the trees, only coming to her knees.

She passed a handful of smaller evergreens that had been broken in two as the car crashed through them, the smell of splintered wood and fresh sap mixing in with the gas.

Sophie stopped twenty feet away.

She was shivering, her hands numb, legs burning with cold.

The engine hissed.

Through the driver-side window, she could see Jim Moreton. Because of the angle of the car, he was lying back in his seat, still strapped in, his head resting unnaturally against his left shoulder.

"Mr. Moreton."

He didn't move.

She stepped closer to the car, now peering in through the rear passenger window. The backseat was empty, the seats soaked with blood. She looked at the windshield—a gaping hole, exploded from within.

Sophie turned and studied the hillside. The twisted guardrail seemed a thousand miles away.

From this perspective, she could see the path the CR-V had taken, punching through the guardrail, then plunging a hundred feet before it hit.

At the second point of impact, she glimpsed a smaller path that branched off and carved down the slope.

It appeared to terminate fifty yards from where she stood at the forest's edge.

She waded through the snow, using the saplings and branches in proximity to keep her upright. Every step was a struggle, and she was sweating after only a minute.

Ten feet out, she spotted the gray of Paige's coat.

She was lying facedown in the snow and there was blood all around her. Sophie bent over and dug two fingers into her carotid.

Twenty feet deeper in the woods, she found Grant.

He was lying on his back.

Eyes open. Not breathing.

Sophie sat down beside him in the snow.

"Look at you," she whispered.

She took his left hand into hers and leaned over and cried.

There would be times in the coming weeks when the numbness would subside and Sophie would remember a cool night in June when she had driven a slightly-too-drunk Grant home from the Stumbling Monk. It was an office party, someone's birthday, and they had spent the evening talking with their knees nearly touching and sometimes touching underneath the bar while the rest of the precinct roared at each other in the booths behind them. This was the night she had surprised herself with her own feelings. After everyone left, she drove him home and they sat in the car outside of Grant's house, their hands so close that the summer breeze coming in through the open windows could have blown them together. She had wanted nothing more than to slide her fingers into his. To hold them. Let them take her inside. But she didn't. And neither did he. That would be the ritual they shared. Two years of walking right up to the door that held everything they wanted, but never opening it. So there would be times in the coming weeks when she would think back to that first moment in the car and how she had been too scared to reach for his hand, and then remember this last one, sitting beside him on a cold foggy morning, when she did.

She had put her job before her love. Before her happiness. Betrayed Grant and herself. She saw it now. Saw it with the kind of scorching clarity that comes like a storm when it's too late to take cover. When there's nothing to be done but face your failing, take the pain, and push on.

Sirens pulled her back into the moment.

They were still miles away, and wailing through the mountains like a tragic anthem.

Sophie started to rise.

At first, she thought it was the light from the rescue party, but it couldn't be with the sirens still too far out, and besides, this light was coming from the sky. From straight overhead. A blinding luminescence hovering just above the trees. Brighter than anything she'd ever witnessed and yet there was no pain, no urge to look away.

As it descended toward her, she lay back in the snow, still holding Grant's hand.

Closer and closer, but no fear.

Only mystery and peace as it finally enveloped her in a sphere of pure light which held some component of familiarity that broke her heart.

Where are you going, Grant?
I don't know yet.
I want to come with you.
It's not your time.
I want to be with you. I always wanted it, but I was too afraid.
I know. I was too.
I'm so sorry.
Have no regret.
Please. I see now. I see everything.
There's still time for us. This is not the end.

She blinked and the light was gone.

Sophie sat up.

She was alone in the forest and her heart was pounding.

That rush of euphoric joy was fading, and she was still holding her partner's cold hand. Time had passed—more than felt right. Up the mountainside, she could see the schizophrenic flashing of the light bars, and there were EMTs and lawmen halfway down the hill.

Already she could feel Sophie-the-skeptic muscling in to discredit what she had just experienced, to undermine it, to subject it to the rigid empiricist that had governed her life up to this moment.

And her first instinct was to listen, to carry on as before.

What has your lack of faith ever done but cause you pain and keep you from the man you love?

No.

Something had happened in these trees.

Something beyond her experience.

Something magic.

She could choose to believe.

Epilogue

Paige is dying.
Paige is five, chewing a piece of spearmint gum.
He's in the CR-V.
His father's '74 Impala.
It's day.
Night.
"Pay attention, guys, you'll remember this game one day."
The guardrail rushes toward them through the fog.
The play-by-play announcer says, "The crowd will tell you what happens."
Paige says, "Daddy?"
Paige moans, "Daddy?"
"Oh shit."
The engine revving.
Grant bracing, realizing neither he nor Paige is buckled in and wondering does it even matter at this point.
Jim says, "Everything will be—"
Straight through.
The engine redlines, goes silent.
Grant can hear the tires spinning underneath him. He and Paige lift off the seat and his head bangs into the ceiling as they plummet. The urge

to hold onto something is overpowering, but he just squeezes Paige, her eyes gone wide.

Don't be scared, Paige.
But I am.
I won't let anything happen to you.
You promise?
I promise.
Swear.
I swear to you, Paige. I'll protect you.

Through the windshield, the white mountainside is screaming toward the front of the car which is now pitched earthward, nothing but g-force pinning Grant to his seat.

He looks down into his sister's eyes a half second before they hit.

Once upon a time, there was a little girl named Paige.
Just like me?
Just like you. And she had an older brother named Grant.
Just like you.
Yes, just like me.
Did they have parents?
No. Paige and Grant lived in a beautiful house all by themselves, and they were very brave.

The sound of metal crumpling.

The shock of snow tearing into the car.

Grant, still clutching Paige, accelerating through the windshield.

And then he is outside, the car flipping beneath him down the hillside in a spray of snow and safety glass.

Paige no longer in his arms and still he's climbing skyward, as high as the tree tops now, the forest falling away beneath him.

The light starts as a pinprick, peeking through the forest below.

It begins to grow.

Slowly at first.

Then faster.

Consuming everything it touches like a fire burning its way through the center of a movie screen. The trees and the fog and the SUV still cartwheeling down the mountain all disappear into its edges, and it seems to Grant that the world is just a shroud for this blinding molten light behind it.

Except for one thing.

Her.

She is below him, crying in the snow.

He is being pulled, but he resists, fighting to descend.

And then he is with her.

The most sensual moment of his existence.

Effortless communication.

Mind to mind.

There is not enough time, but he makes every word, every second count.

He is ripped away.

And then…

Dad? Are you there?

I'm here.

It's so bright.

Don't close your eyes. Look right at it. No matter what.

I can't feel anything.

That will pass. Just keep watching.

The light is everywhere and it touches everything. He feels his body blown away from him like sand. Old and new pain leaving.

The light begins to splinter. To condense into pinpoints. Beyond counting.

Are those stars?

It is Paige. Not her voice. But her.

Some of them.

Is that where we're going?

If you want to. We can go anywhere you want.

Can we see Mom?

Yes. And others.

I don't understand.

You will.

Then all at once, those pinpoints of light stretch toward them, as if they've been summoned.

The children hesitate, the stars streaming past like whitewater.
It is their father who pulls them forward.
Come on, they're waiting for us.
There's nothing to be afraid of anymore.

THE END

Bonus Features

Afterword

In Which Blake and Jordan Interview Each Other About the Experience of Writing EERIE

Blake: For pretty much everybody except me, EERIE is their first taste of Jordan Crouch. Hmm. That didn't sound quite right. How about you just introduce yourself?

Jordan: Hi, I'm the younger brother.

Blake: By six years.

Jordan: More?

Blake: Um, yeah.

Jordan: Hi, I'm the handsome younger brother. I graduated from the University of North Carolina Wilmington in 2007 with degrees in Creative Writing and English Lit. This is my first endgame. Seattle, Washington, is home and when I'm not thinking of answers to hypothetical interview questions, I operate as a splinter cell for the Department of Homeland Security. You're welcome, America.

Blake: What do you really do?

Jordan: I work in sales.

Blake: You've always been one of my first readers for my books, because you've got a great sense of story, without being married to the more conventional plot machinations. I guess what I'm trying to say is, I think you and I share some overlapping DNA (imagine that) in terms of the sort of big, different ideas that attract us. You've also come up with some real crunch time story fixes for me over the years. Probably the most epic example of that is the end of my historical thriller, ABANDON. I was really at a loss about how to wrap that book up and you came up with a fantastic idea ... don't want to ruin it here for those readers who haven't picked it up yet, but the epilogue was totally your idea.

I love the collaboration process, and despite the fact that you hadn't written a novel, always loved your writing, so I thought it only made sense for you and I to work together one day. Then last fall, you hit me with a kickass premise ...

Jordan: To give credit where credit is due, the kernel that bloomed into this buttery piece of popcorn came from a close friend of mine named Bob. We've known each other for years, and his brain works at least twice as fast as mine so he often ends up being a sounding board for story ideas. The "monster-in-the-bedroom" premise happened during a phone conversation at the beginning 2011. In its earliest birth pains, it was about two hunters snowed in at a cabin with "something" locked in the bedroom. Then you and I ruined it.

Blake: Yeah, I flipped when you told me about it. It truly was just a kernel, but it struck me as something I hadn't heard before. And possibly as a vehicle to write a type of story I had never attempted: a ghost story (although by now, our readers know EERIE was only dressed up like a ghost story). But what attracted me initially to the concept was how confined in space and time it was, and with minimal characters. Almost like a play. I just thought it had tremendous potential. After that first conversation, I brought it up a month later (it really stuck with me), asking if you and

Bob were going to write it. You said no, and then I asked if you might want to write it with me.

Jordan: That was a no-brainer. It was a dynamite idea that needed to be written, and I would have been happy to see you tackle it by yourself. But the idea of working together is what put it over the edge for me.

Blake: Now I've written ten novels and a ton of short stories and novellas. I've collaborated with half a dozen people. You had written some short fiction in college and after, but this was pretty much your first foray both into a novel-length work and into collaboration. Spare no punches. How was the process for you? The good, the bad, and the ugly?

ASIDE: Before you answer, for those interested, the way we wrote this was a mix of real time Google Docs writing (you and I writing simultaneously in the same document) and then you and I working on scenes in isolation and sharing them later. We also spent about a month hammering out characters and a 5000-word outline which served as our roadmap (although we were allowed to take detours, and often did).

Jordan: I want to say first that I walked into this knowing that it was a golden ticket learning opportunity, and that whatever happened, the value of the experience would outweigh any of the bumps or bruises along the way. I don't take for granted how lucky I am to love writing and also to have a brother who has built a career around it. But all modest stuff aside, the hardest part was trying not to step on your toes, while still attempting to plant my flag on the story. It was like sharing a room together again. Sometimes that claustrophobia would show up on the page, and I would watch you strike something that I really liked and think "Are you kidding me? That's the best part!" But that's how you make a cohesive voice in a collaborative story. You each hold your own light up to the other's work and hope it evens out.

Blake: Apt analogy, but you did far more than plant your flag. I would say most of the important plot moves came from you.

Jordan: I'll have to check the scoreboard. I do wonder if you would have been as ruthless if I weren't your brother.

Blake: Definitely not. And you bore my ruthlessness with total grace.

Jordan: You mentioned earlier that we wrote most of EERIE simultaneously, in real time, using Google Docs. That was a tough learning experience too. You tend to think of writing as this very personal, monastic thing you do alone with the door shut, but when you're forced to share the page with someone else, it exercises muscles you would never use otherwise. There's a lot of pressure to keep the pace going and to stay out of your head which is an easy rut to get stuck in if there's no one staring back at you from the other side of the screen.

Blake: The most challenging aspect of this collaboration for me was our familiarity. When I've worked with past collaborators, even though (with some exceptions) I know them fairly well, everyone is still pretty much on their best behavior. But you and I are brothers. We love each other, we have a blast together, but there are also times when we fight, when we annoy the shit out of each other. So there were some occasions, on both ends, when we lost our cool and said things we wouldn't have said to people who weren't kin.

Jordan: I only remember apologizing to you once. But I'm sure there were other times I should have. So sorry or whatever.

Blake: Whenever we fought, it was always about the story. About wanting it to be as good as it could possibly be. And every time, we rallied, and truthfully there were only a handful of times when I wanted to throw my laptop at you.

One other thing ... even though it's a brother/sister relationship, the heart of this story is a sibling relationship. In the outline process, we didn't realize Paige and Grant were brother and sister until very late in the game, but now that the book is done, I find it strange we didn't come to it sooner. There were a few moments between them when I felt very strongly that we were channeling some of our dynamics (me trying to get you out of the male prostitution game) but seriously, it was kind of surreal. In the end, I believe it made for a far more intense emotional impact on the page than if I had been writing with someone else.

Jordan: Yeah, it's pretty funny that two siblings couldn't figure out that they should be writing a story about two siblings. Originally, Grant was going to be this infatuated suitor who discovers that Paige, his high school crush, has suddenly breezed back into town. It's gross now, and it didn't work then either. It made Grant feel weak and Paige seem manipulative. You were the one who suggested the brother/sister angle. We were on the phone and you mentioned it in passing like it would never work, but as soon as you said it, it was obvious that it couldn't be any other way.

Blake: I'm already getting sentimental about our time writing together and wondering how long it will be before we get to do it again. Any successful collaboration is an amazing experience, but to be able to share it with your brother really makes it special.

Jordan: As a kid, I always wanted to be doing whatever you were doing. Anyone who has an older brother that they don't hate will tell you that feeling never changes. You grow up, but you still want your big bro to be proud of you. I said earlier that the value of the experience was in how much I learned. But that's not even half the story. The best part was spending time with you, doing something we're both passionate about.

Blake: Back at you, bro. So what are you working on after EERIE, and when will you have a solo project to share with the world?

Jordan: EERIER. Kidding. I have a few short stories lined up, and another novel that should be out later this year. What about you?

Blake: We've talked about that novel, and it's an AMAZING idea. My next novel, PINES, is coming out through Amazon's Thomas & Mercer imprint on August 28, 2012. Really, really psyched about that one. Like EERIE, it's a bit of a departure for me, a side that I don't think people have seen before, and it has the biggest twist ending/reveal I've ever written.

Jordan: I've read it and at the risk turning this into a circle jerk, it's my favorite thing you've done. I feel like it's the story you've been wanting to write since our parents made the mistake of letting you watch Twin Peaks at the tender age of twelve.

Blake: They had no idea what it would end up doing to me.

Well, as I write this, it's midnight on March 22, 2012, and the book is technically not finished. We're at the point where Paige and Grant are about to arrive at the cabin, and as they say, "all will be revealed." It's possible we're doing this interview to procrastinate from actually writing, but I have a feeling it's because we know the end is very close, and now that all the hard stuff is behind us, we don't want it to end. At least, that's how I feel. Let's go finish this thing. Love you, bro, and until next time!

About the Authors

BLAKE CROUCH is the author of ten novels and numerous short stories, including RUN, DESERT PLACES, STIRRED, and the SERIAL series.

WWW.BLAKECROUCH.COM

JORDAN CROUCH was born in the piedmont of North Carolina in 1984. He attended the University of North Carolina at Wilmington and graduated in 2007 with a degree in Creative Writing. Jordan lives in Seattle, Washington. EERIE is his first novel.

WWW.AUTHORJORDANCROUCH.COM

Blake Crouch's Full Catalog

Andrew Z. Thomas thrillers

Desert Places

Locked Doors

Break You

Stirred

Thicker Than Blood

Other works

Run

Pines

Eerie with Jordan Crouch

Draculas with J.A. Konrath, Jeff Strand, and F. Paul Wilson

Abandon

Snowbound

Famous

Perfect Little Town (horror novella)

Bad Girl (short story)

Serial with Jack Kilborn

Serial Uncut with J.A. Konrath and Jack Kilborn

Killers with Jack Kilborn

Killers Uncut with Jack Kilborn

Serial Killers Uncut with Jack Kilborn and J.A. Konrath

Birds of Prey with Jack Kilborn and J.A. Konrath

Hunting Season: A Love Story with Selena Kitt

Shining Rock (short story)

*69 (short story)
On the Good, Red Road (short story)
Remaking (short story)
The Meteorologist (short story)
The Pain of Others (novella)
Unconditional (short story)
Four Live Rounds (collected stories)
Six in the Cylinder (collected stories)
Fully Loaded (complete collected stories)

Visit Blake at WWW.BLAKECROUCH.COM

Coming Soon

Pines by Blake Crouch
Sunset Key by Blake Crouch
Wolfmen by Crouch, Kitt, Konrath & Leather

Printed in Great Britain
by Amazon

54301536R00159